5118
6.99

✓ **W9-AWD-662**

THIS COMIC
BELONGS TO:

Disney

MICKEY AND THE ROADSTER RACERS

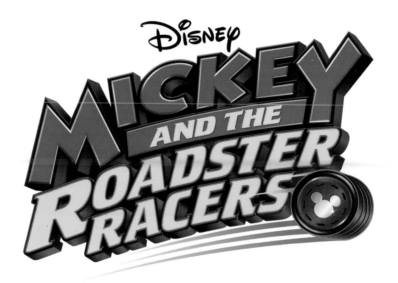

Published simultaneously in the United States and Canada by Joe Books Ltd,
489 College Street, Suite 203, Toronto, ON M6G 1A5

www.joebooks.com

First Joe Books edition: October 2017

Print ISBN: 978-1-77275-560-2
ebook ISBN: 978-1-77275-823-8

Library and Archives Canada Cataloguing in Publication
information is available upon request

Printed and bound in Canada
1 3 5 7 9 10 8 6 4 2

Disney

MICKEY AND THE ROADSTER RACERS

RUNNING OF THE ROADSTERS

CINESTORY COMIC

JOE BOOKS LTD

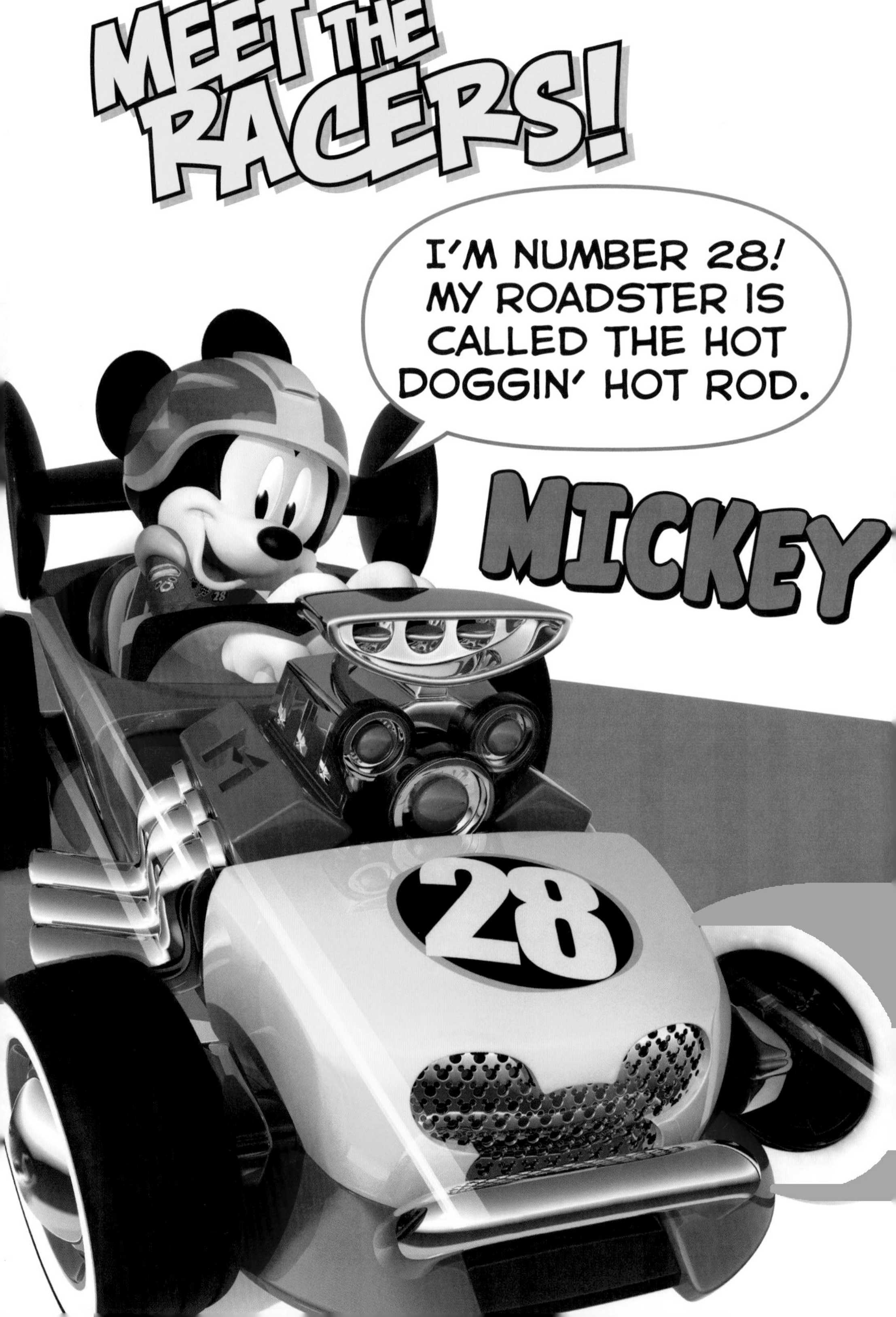
MEET THE RACERS!
I'M NUMBER 28! MY ROADSTER IS CALLED THE HOT DOGGIN' HOT ROD.
MICKEY
28

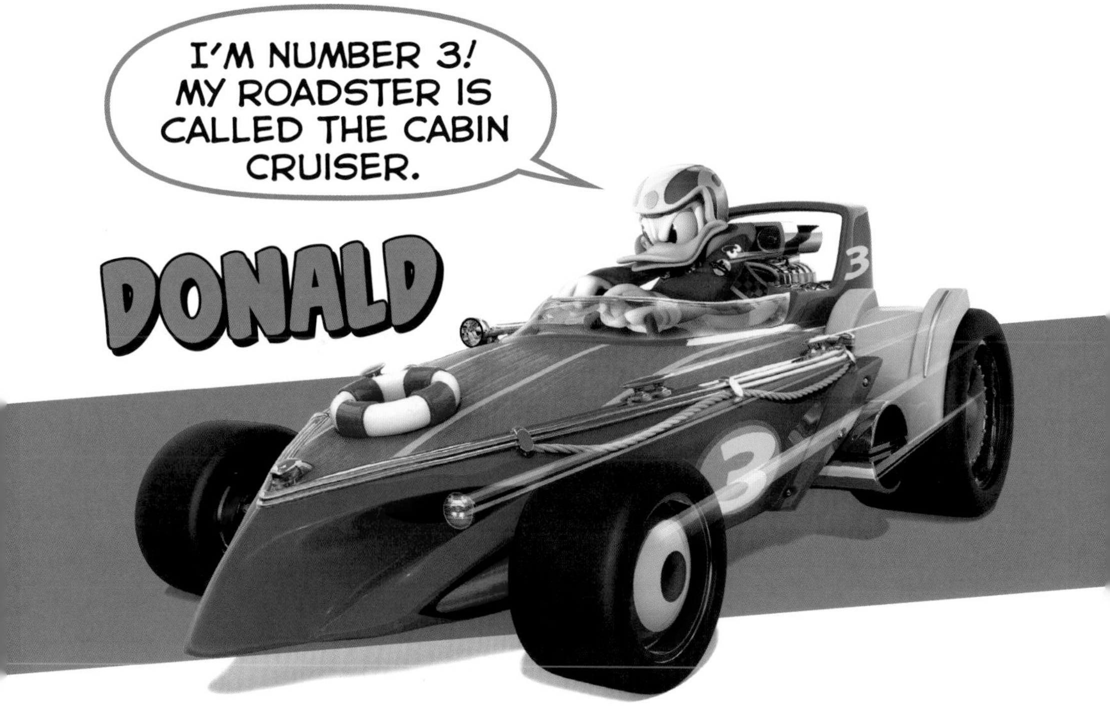
I'M NUMBER 3! MY ROADSTER IS CALLED THE CABIN CRUISER.
DONALD

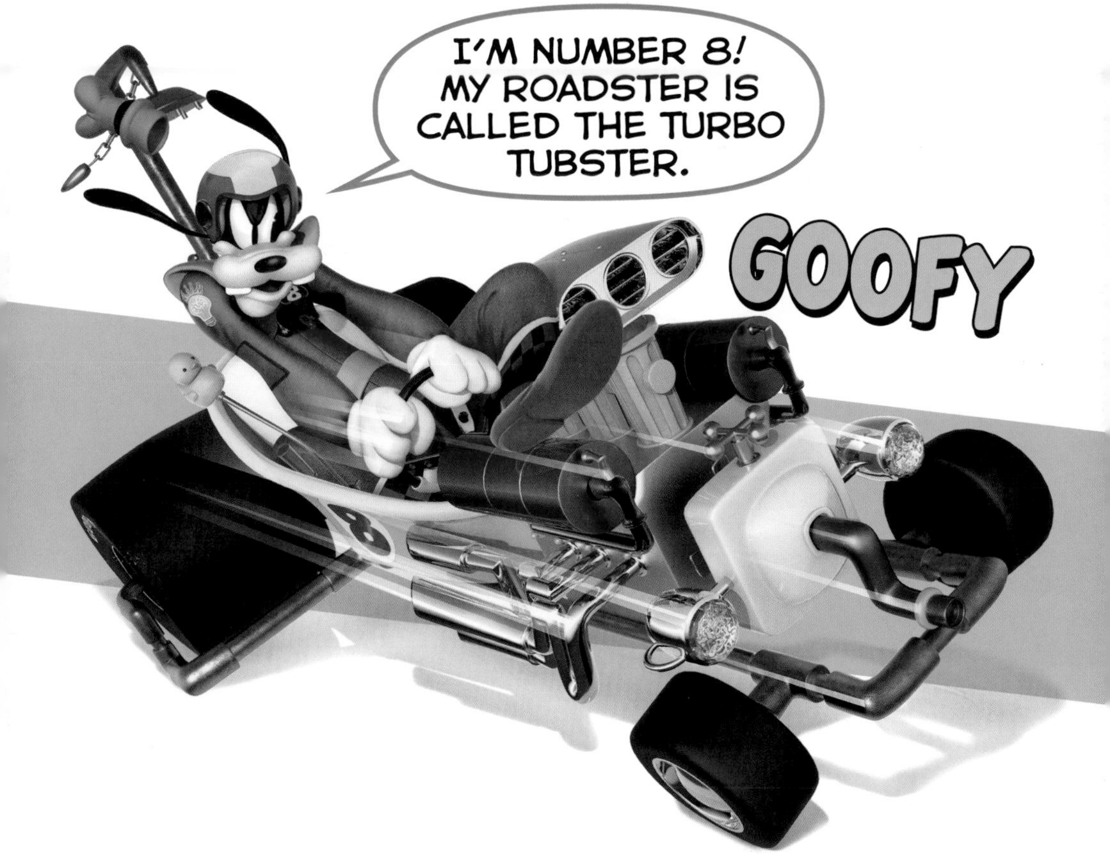
I'M NUMBER 8! MY ROADSTER IS CALLED THE TURBO TUBSTER.
GOOFY

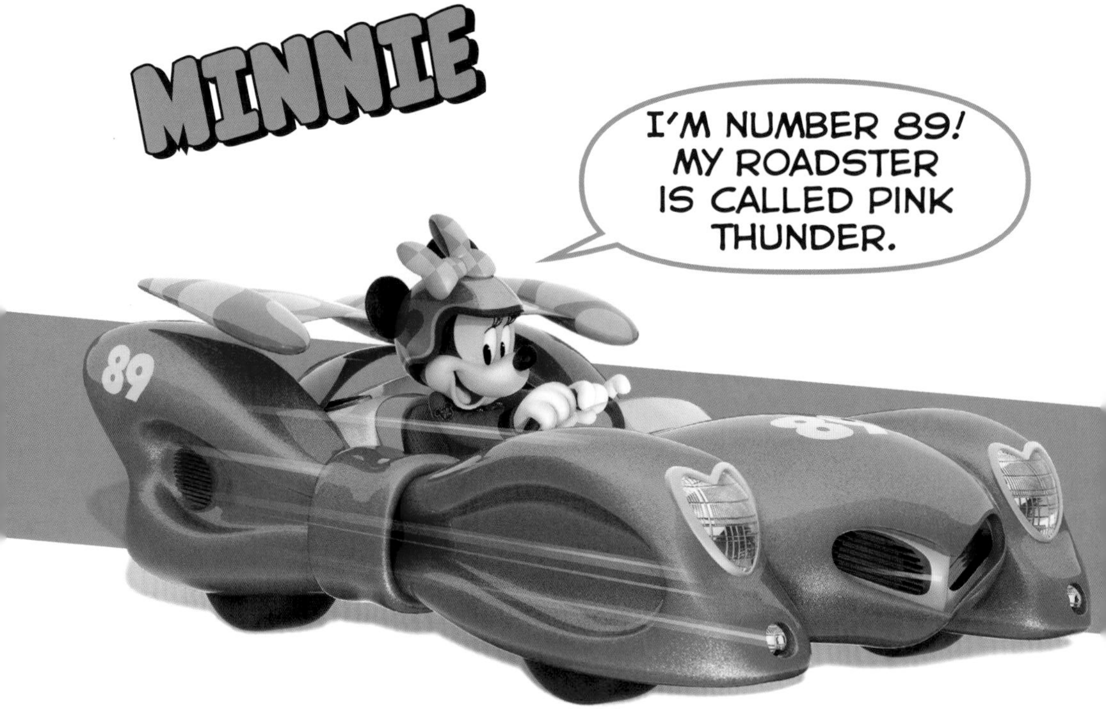
MINNIE
I'M NUMBER 89! MY ROADSTER IS CALLED PINK THUNDER.
89

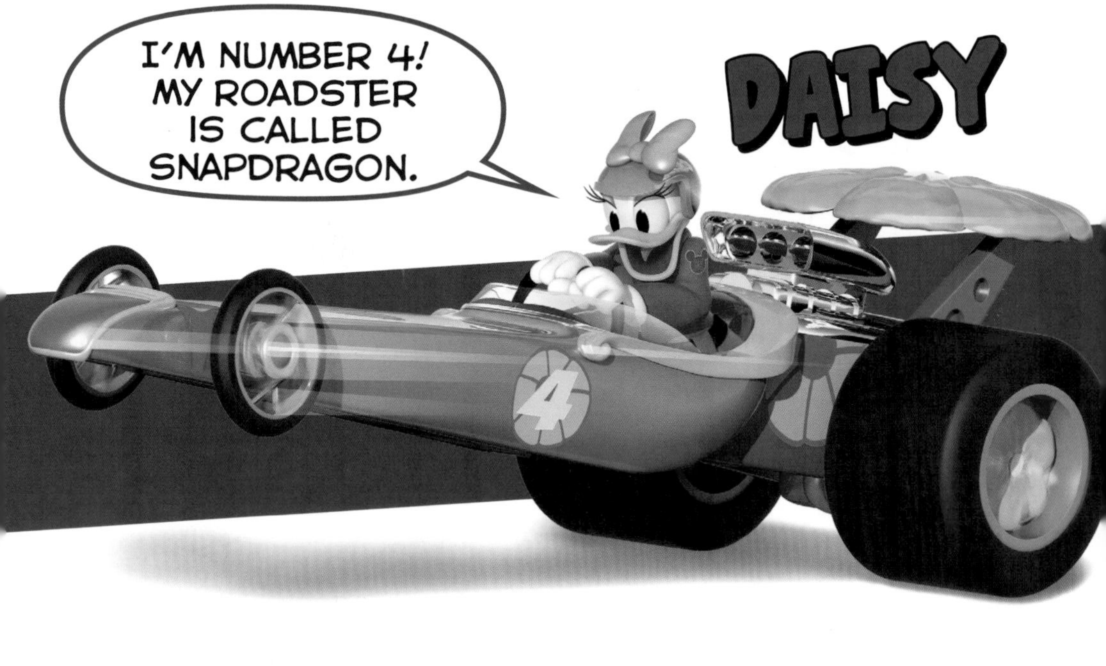
I'M NUMBER 4! MY ROADSTER IS CALLED SNAPDRAGON.
DAISY
4

Disney Mickey and the Roadster Racers

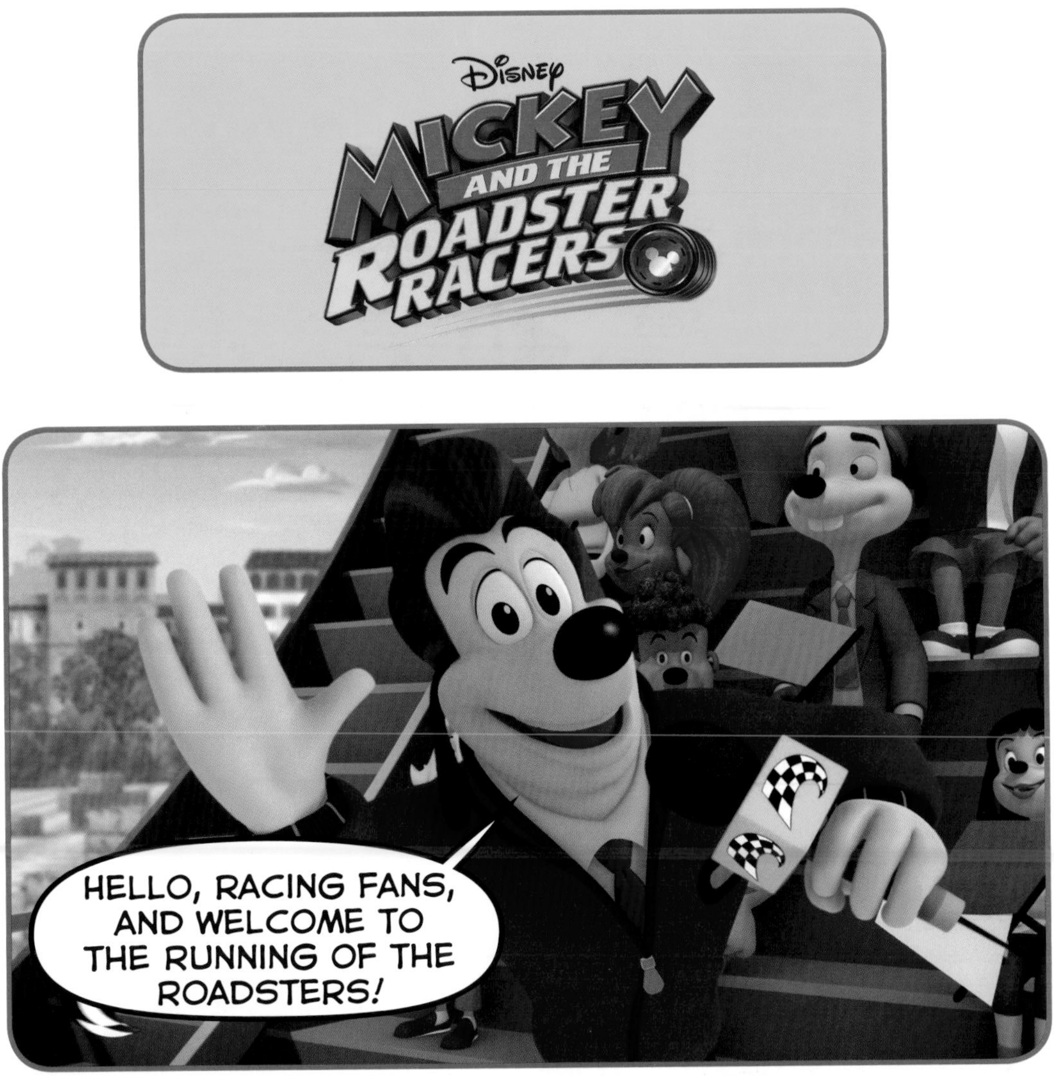
HELLO, RACING FANS, AND WELCOME TO THE RUNNING OF THE ROADSTERS!

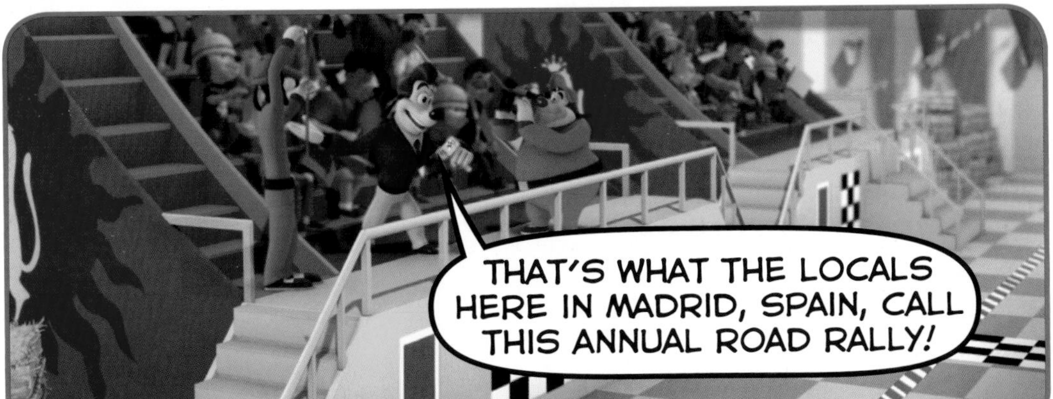
THAT'S WHAT THE LOCALS HERE IN MADRID, SPAIN, CALL THIS ANNUAL ROAD RALLY!

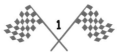

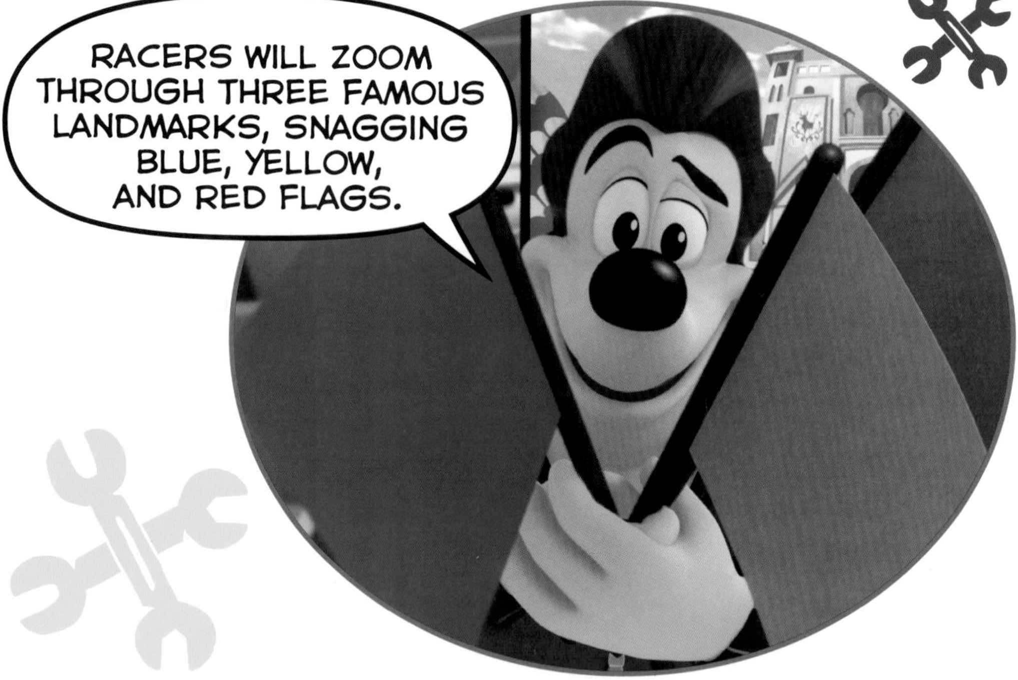
RACERS WILL ZOOM THROUGH THREE FAMOUS LANDMARKS, SNAGGING BLUE, YELLOW, AND RED FLAGS.

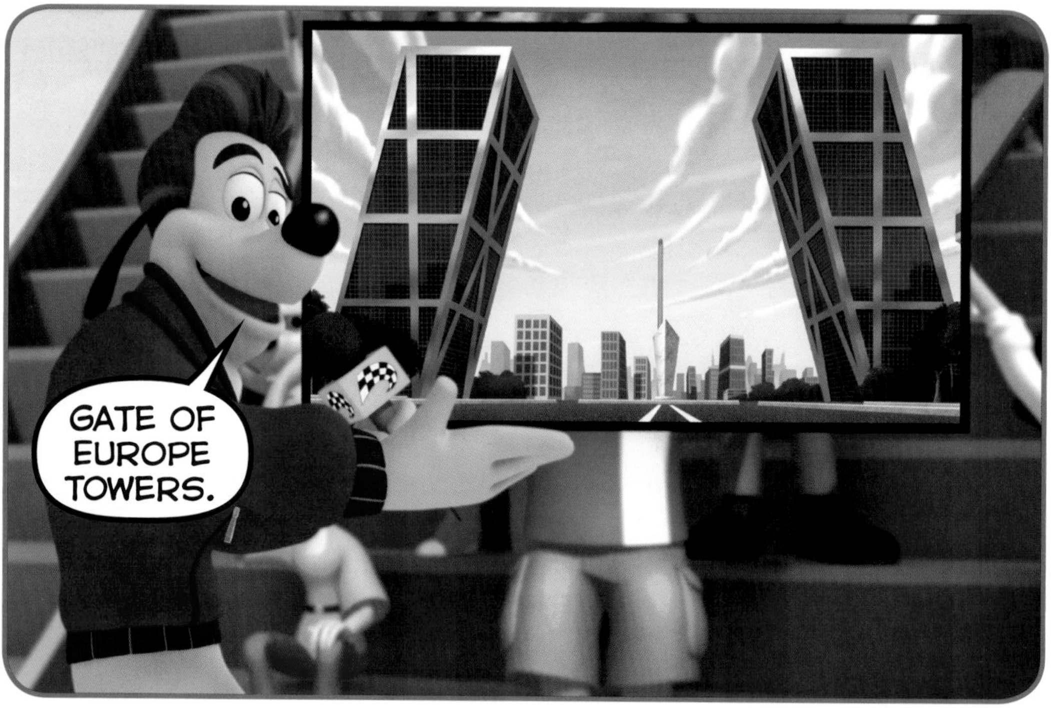
GATE OF EUROPE TOWERS.

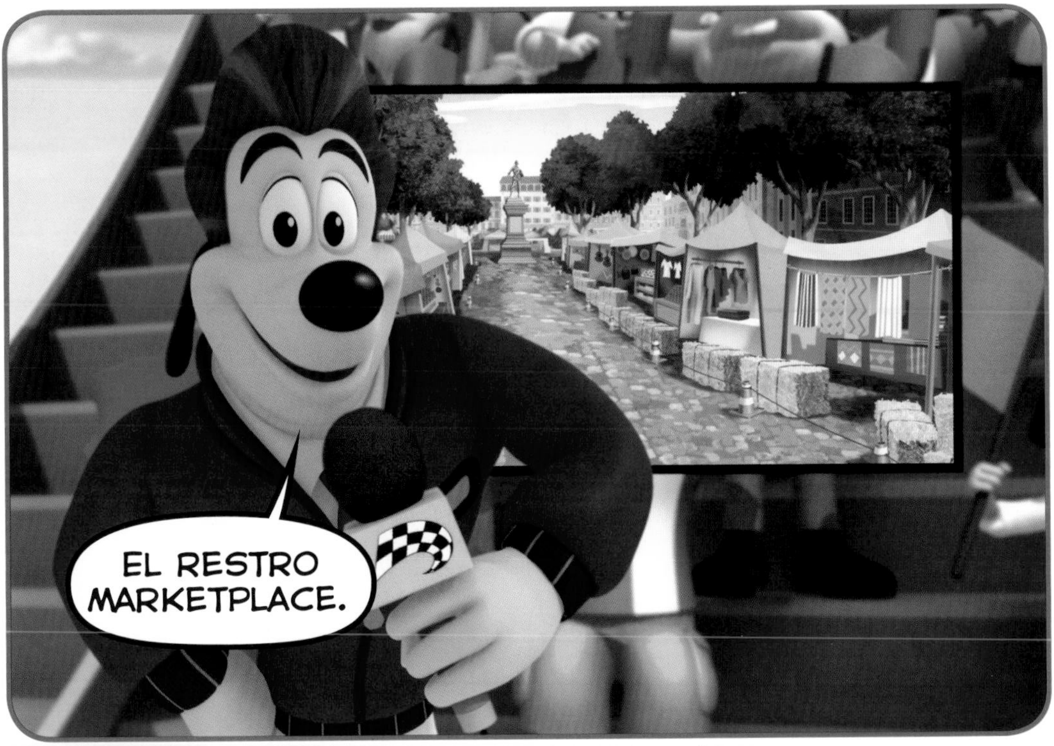
EL RESTRO MARKETPLACE.

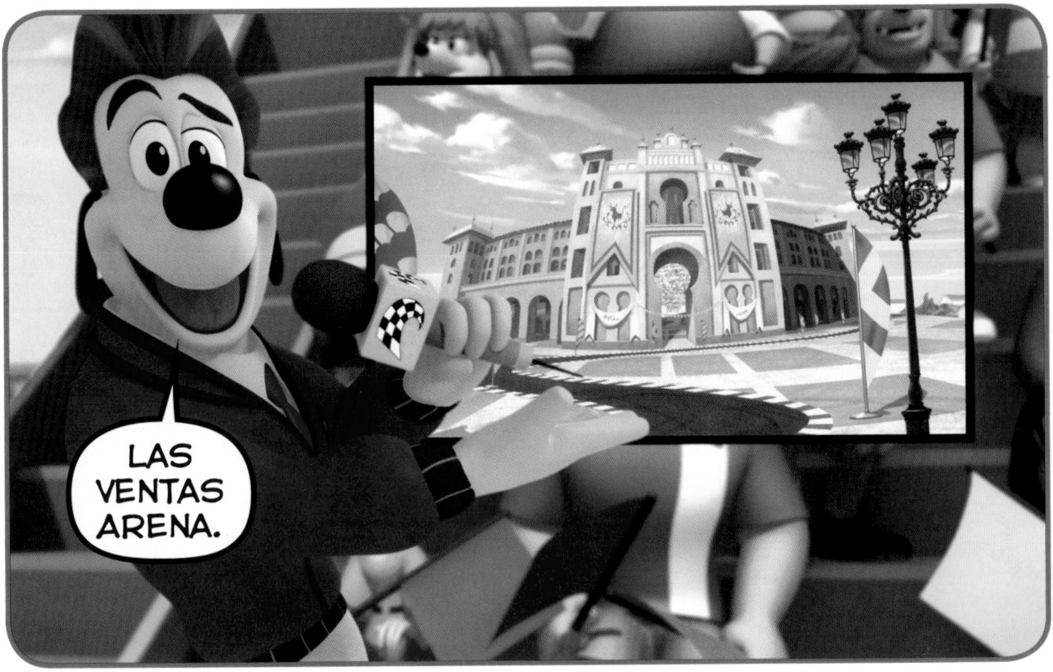
LAS VENTAS ARENA.

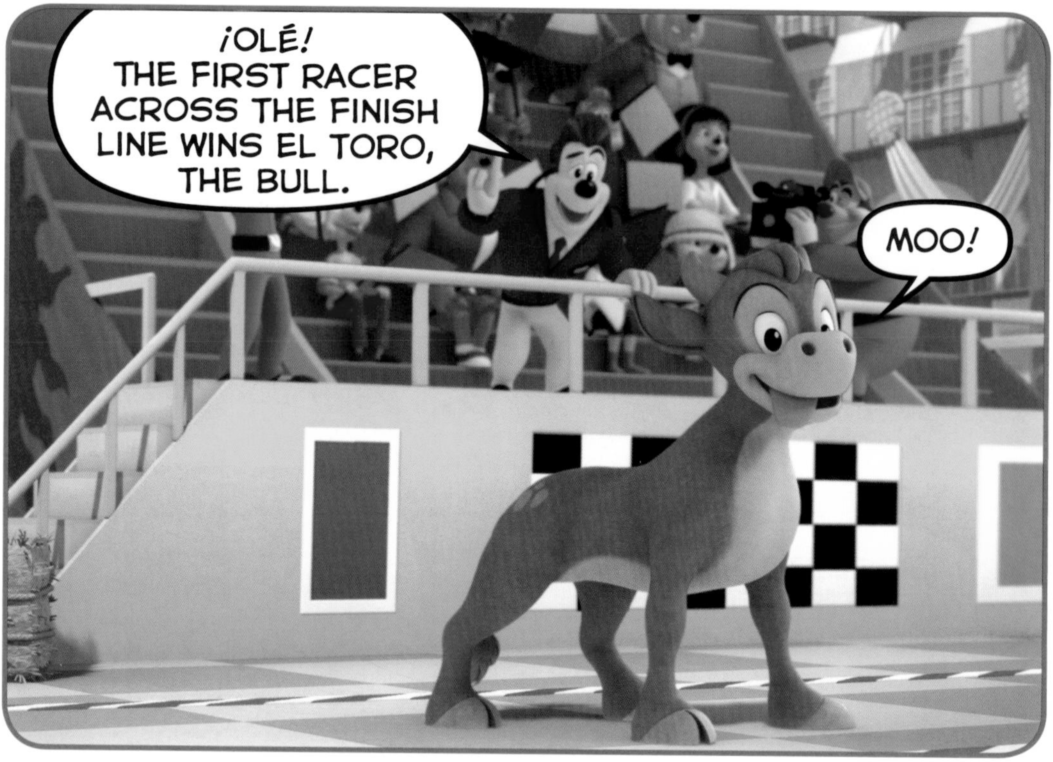
¡OLÉ!
THE FIRST RACER ACROSS THE FINISH LINE WINS EL TORO, THE BULL.
MOO!

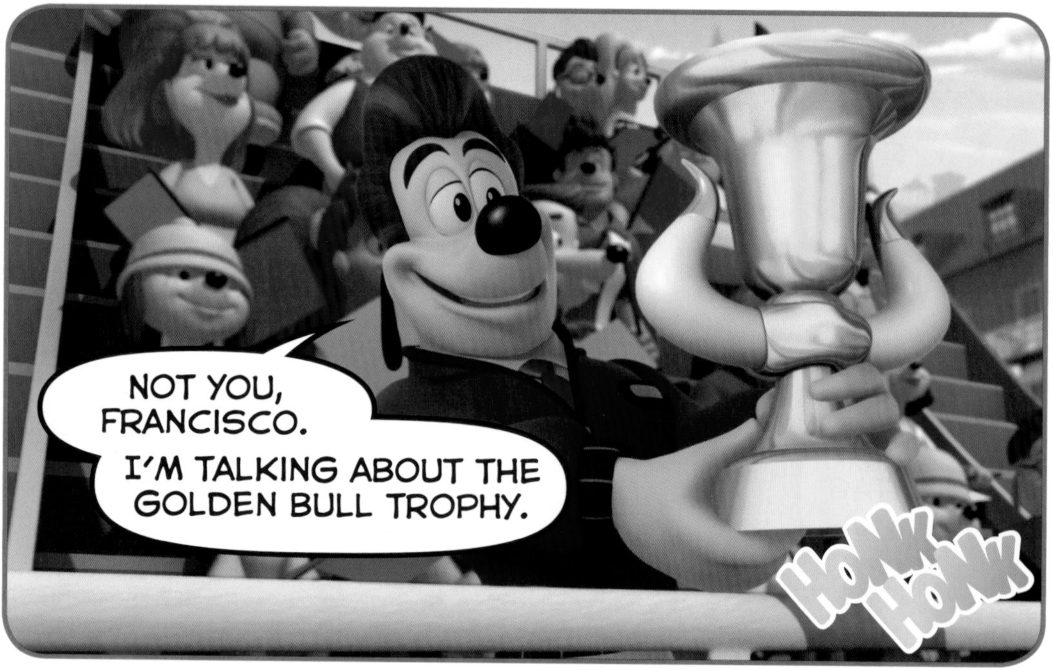
NOT YOU, FRANCISCO.
I'M TALKING ABOUT THE GOLDEN BULL TROPHY.
HONK HONK

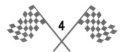

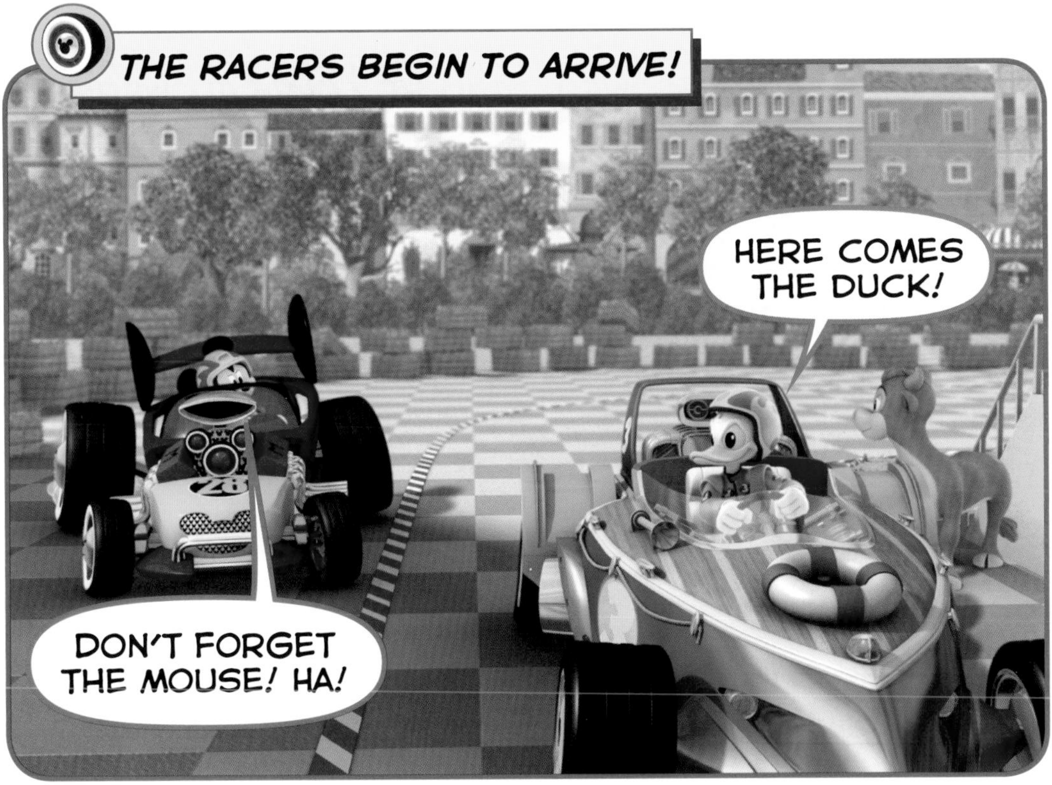
THE RACERS BEGIN TO ARRIVE!
HERE COMES THE DUCK!
DON'T FORGET THE MOUSE! HA!

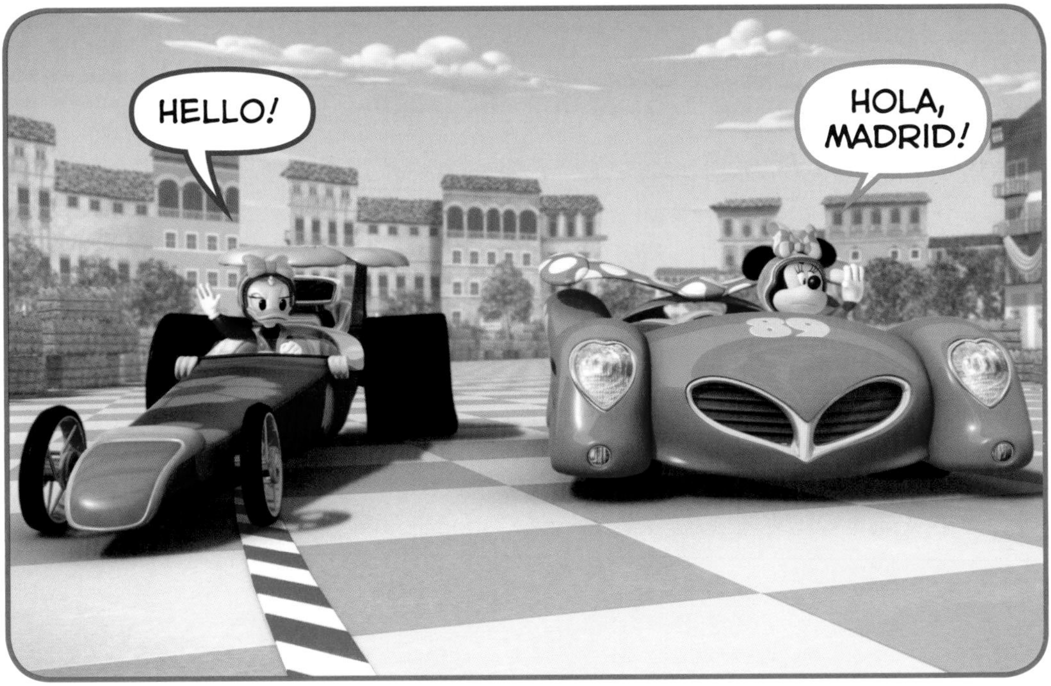
HELLO!
HOLA, MADRID!

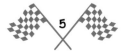

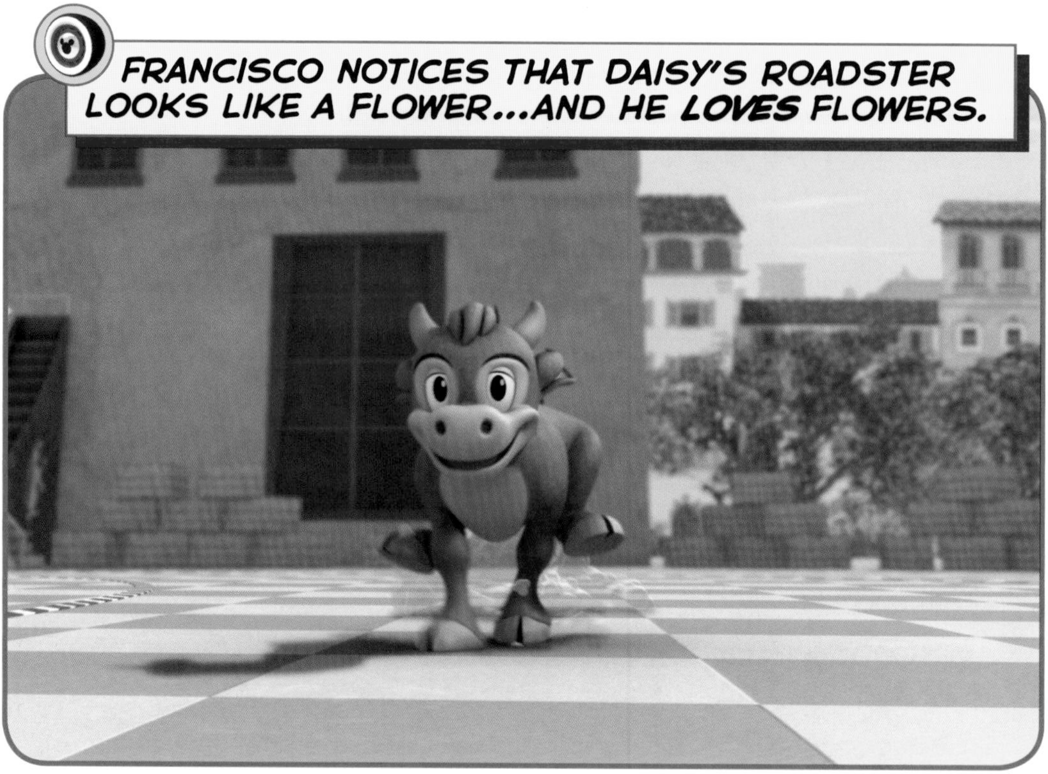
FRANCISCO NOTICES THAT DAISY'S ROADSTER LOOKS LIKE A FLOWER...AND HE *LOVES* FLOWERS.

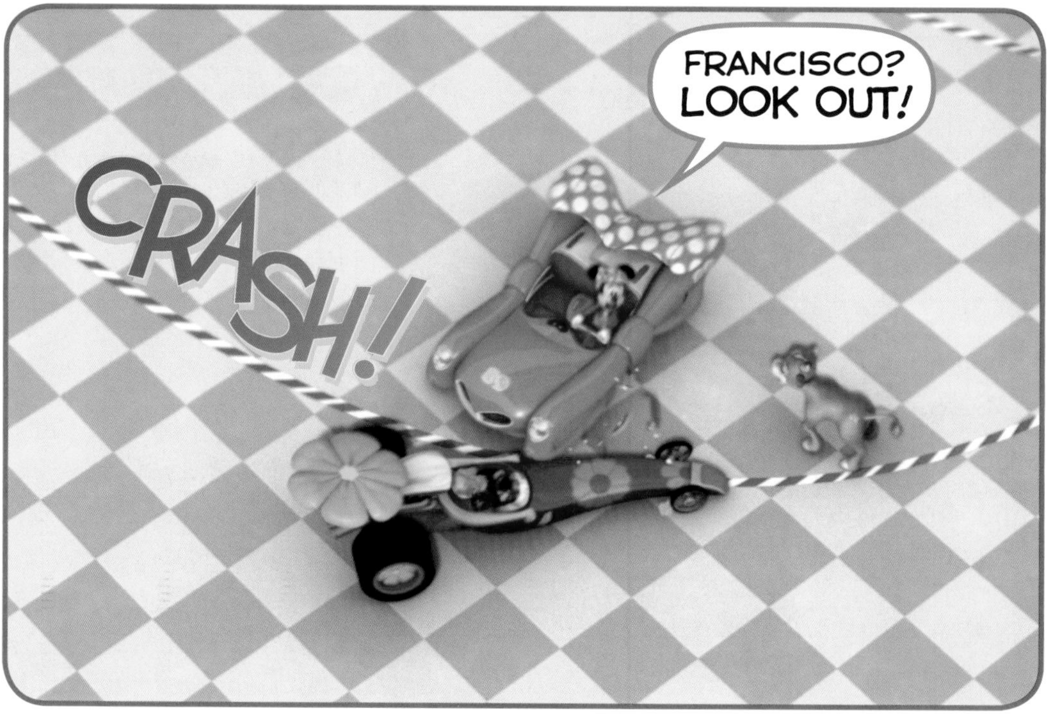
FRANCISCO? LOOK OUT!
CRASH!

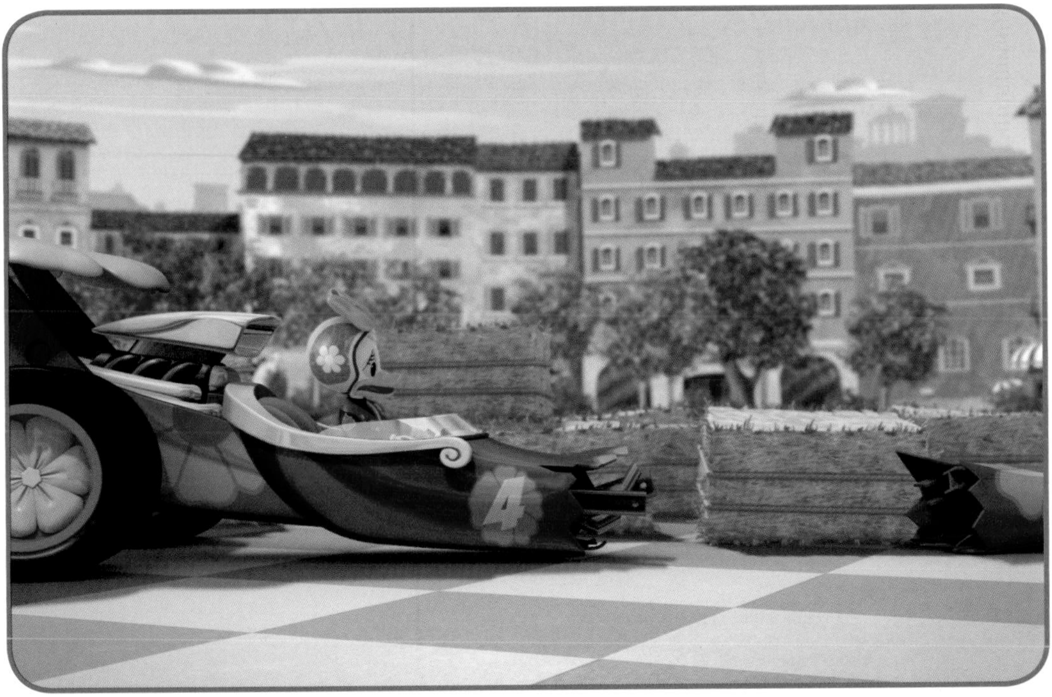

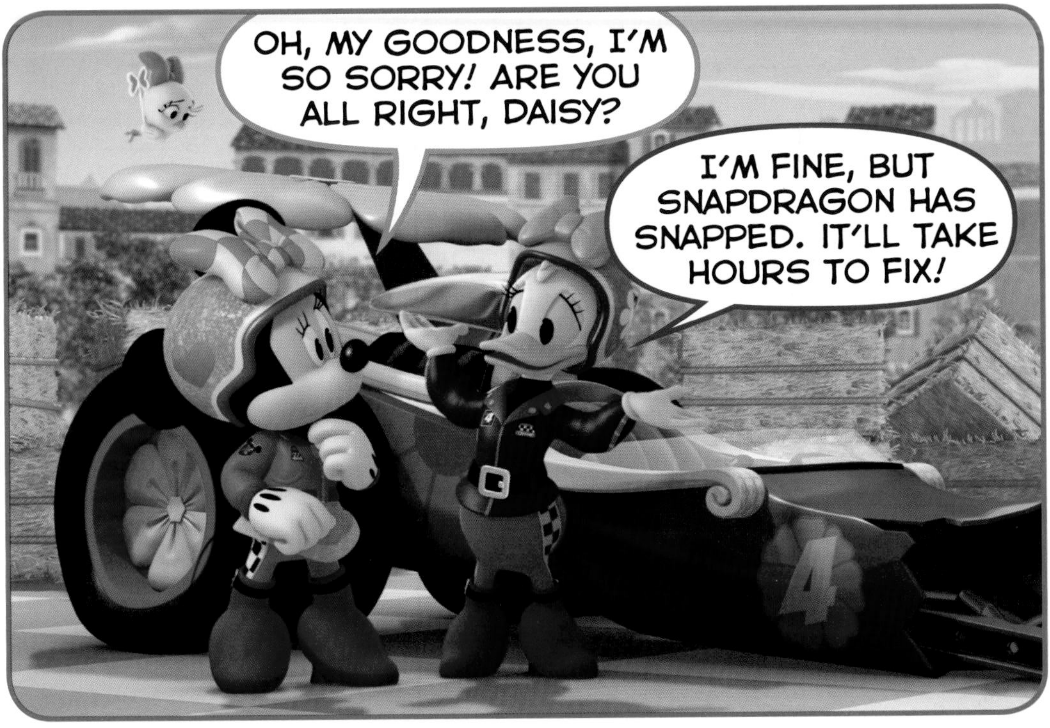
OH, MY GOODNESS, I'M SO SORRY! ARE YOU ALL RIGHT, DAISY?
I'M FINE, BUT SNAPDRAGON HAS SNAPPED. IT'LL TAKE HOURS TO FIX!

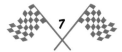

MINNIE'S ROADSTER TURNS INTO THE HAPPY HELPERS VAN.

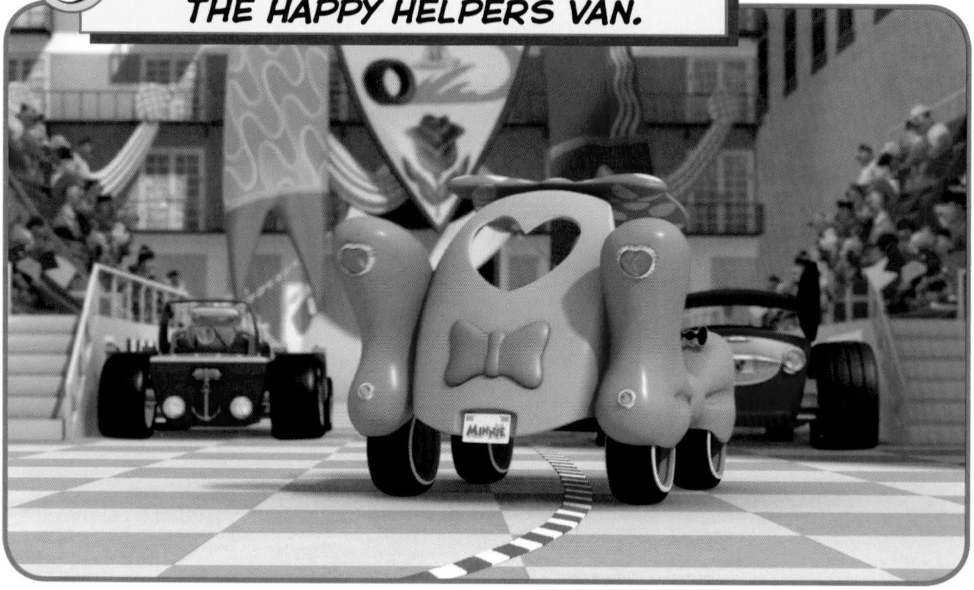
MINNIE

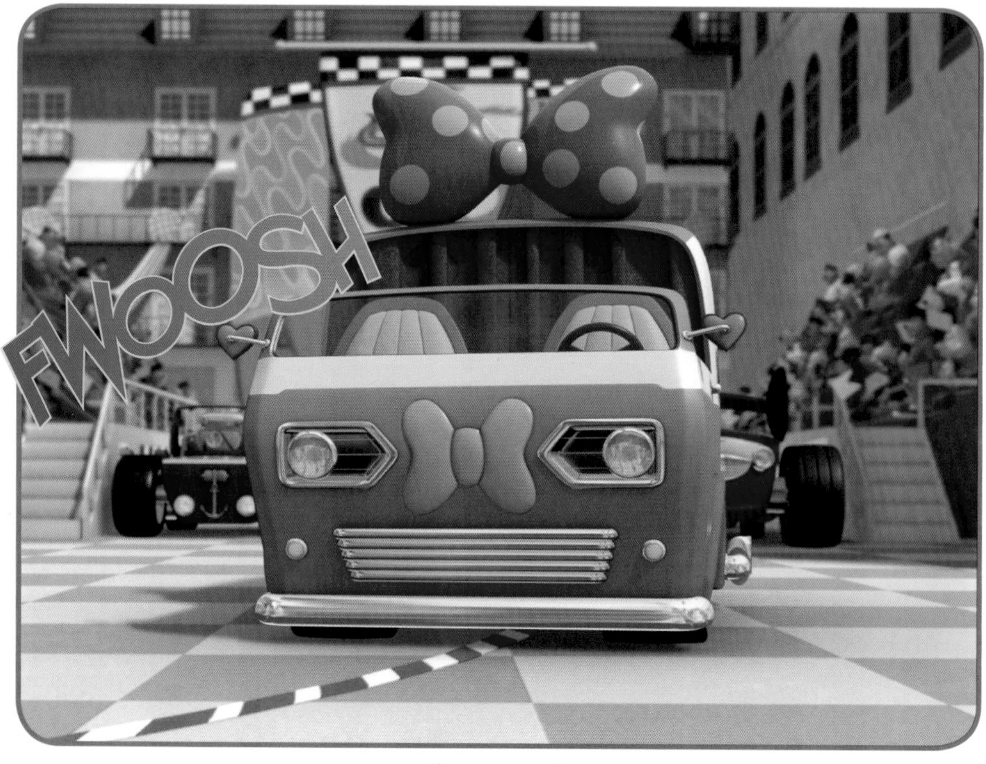
FWOOSH

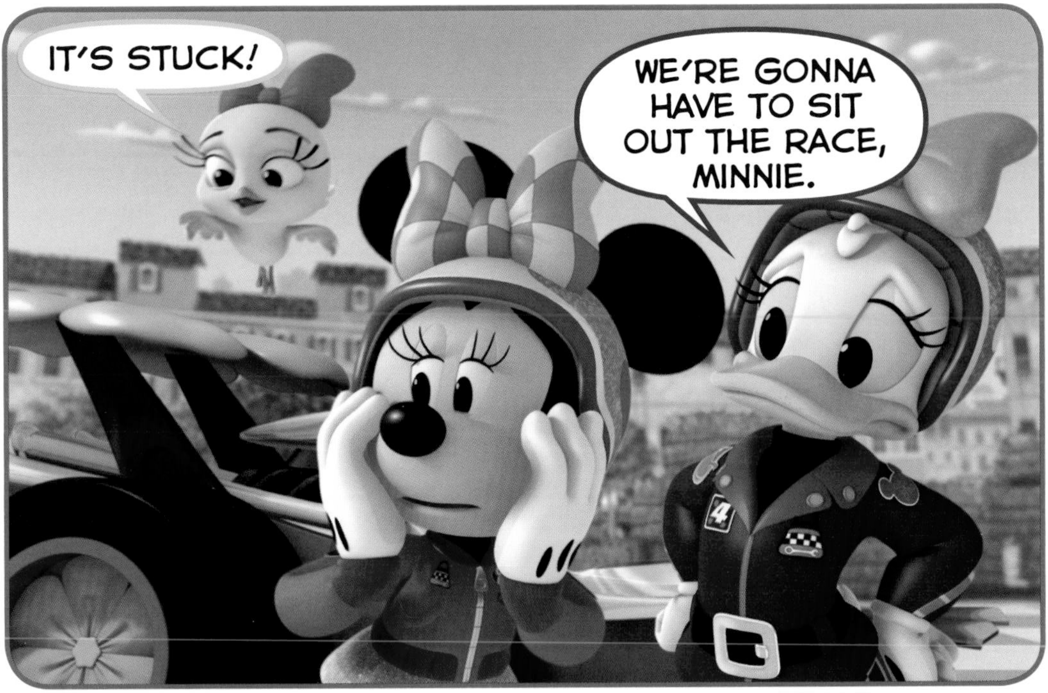
IT'S STUCK!
WE'RE GONNA HAVE TO SIT OUT THE RACE, MINNIE.

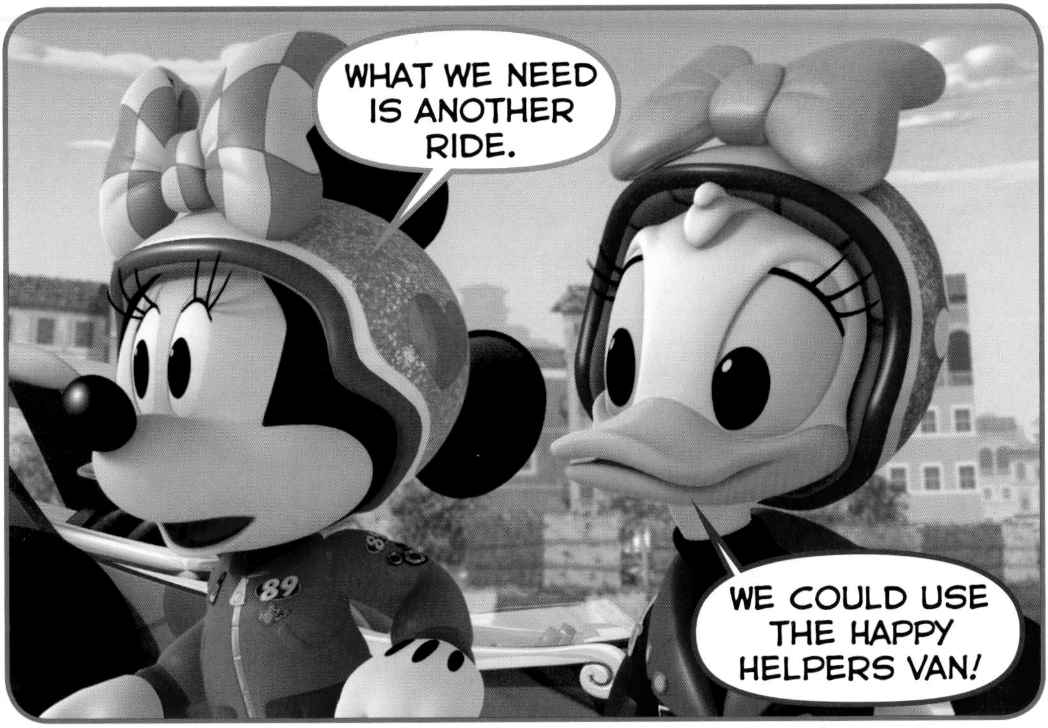
WHAT WE NEED IS ANOTHER RIDE.
WE COULD USE THE HAPPY HELPERS VAN!

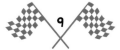

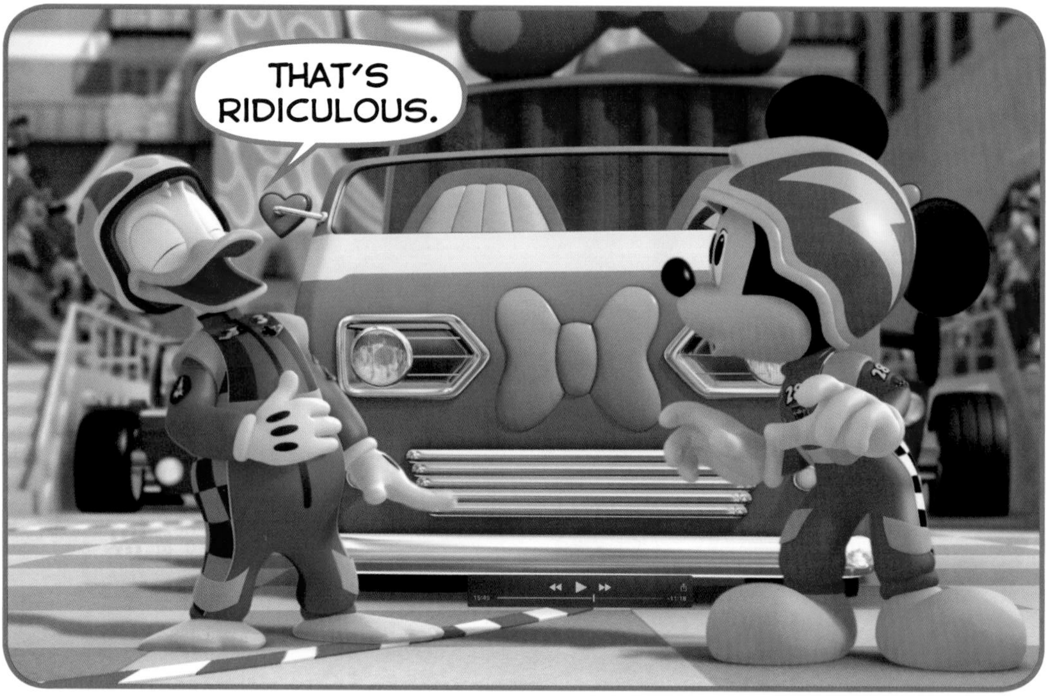
THAT'S RIDICULOUS.

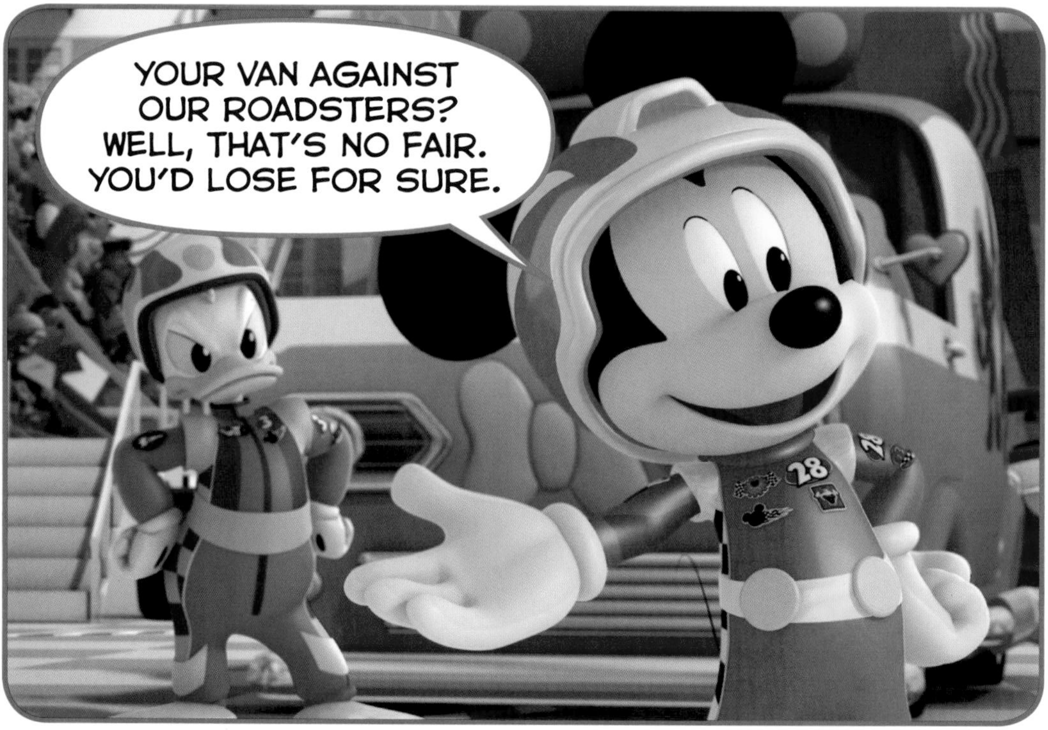
YOUR VAN AGAINST OUR ROADSTERS? WELL, THAT'S NO FAIR. YOU'D LOSE FOR SURE.

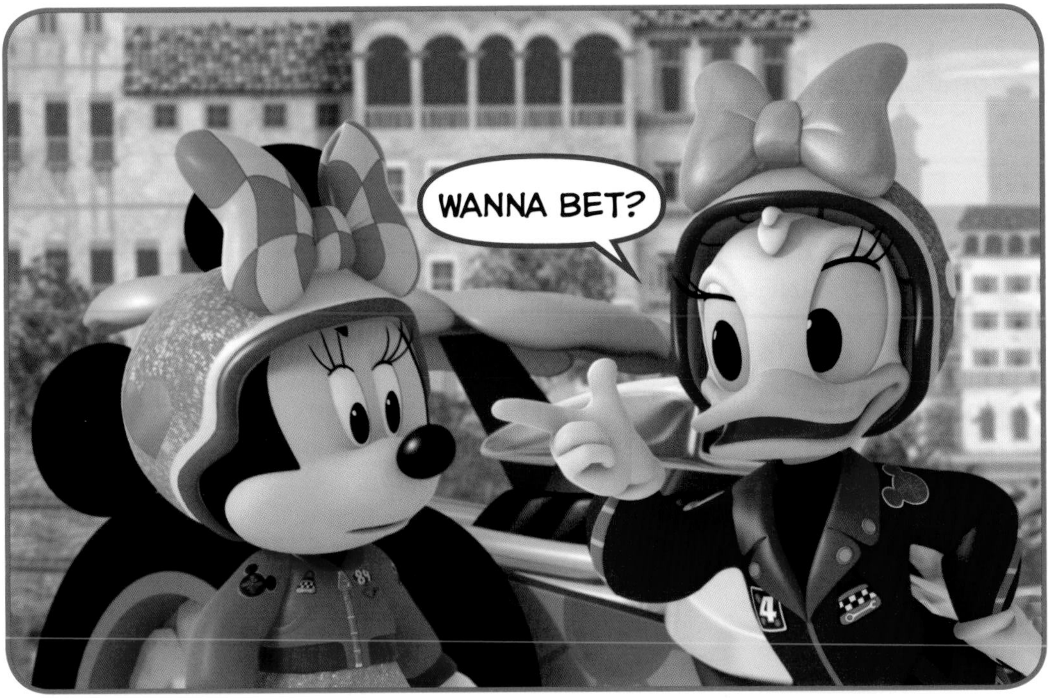
WANNA BET?

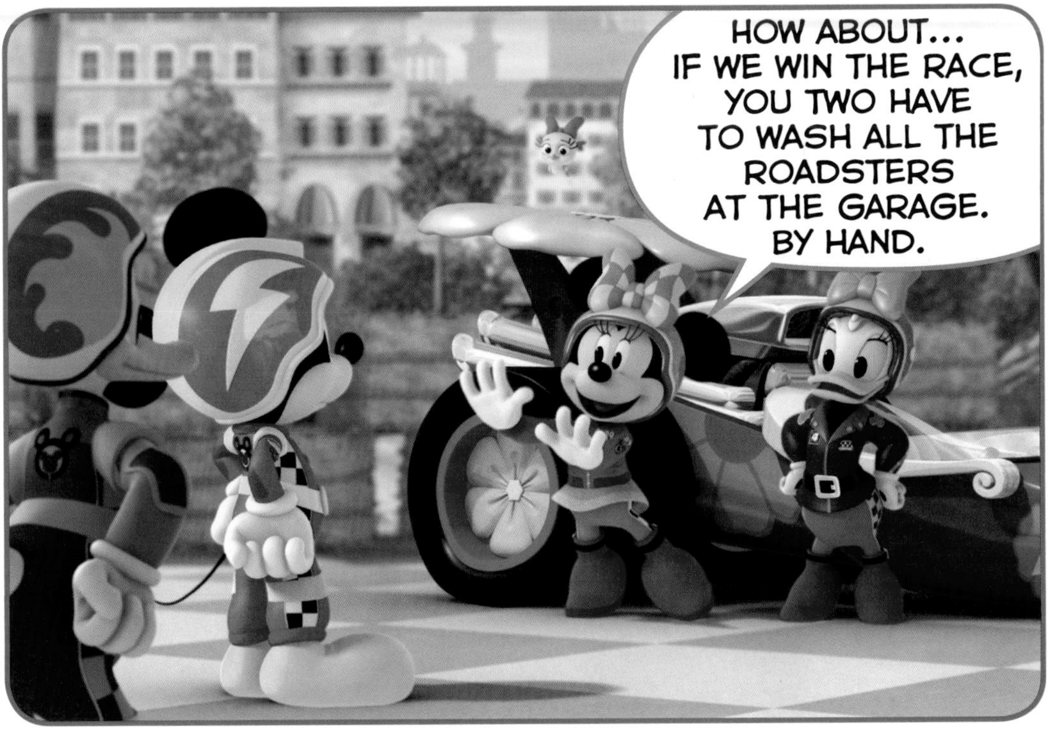
HOW ABOUT... IF WE WIN THE RACE, YOU TWO HAVE TO WASH ALL THE ROADSTERS AT THE GARAGE. BY HAND.

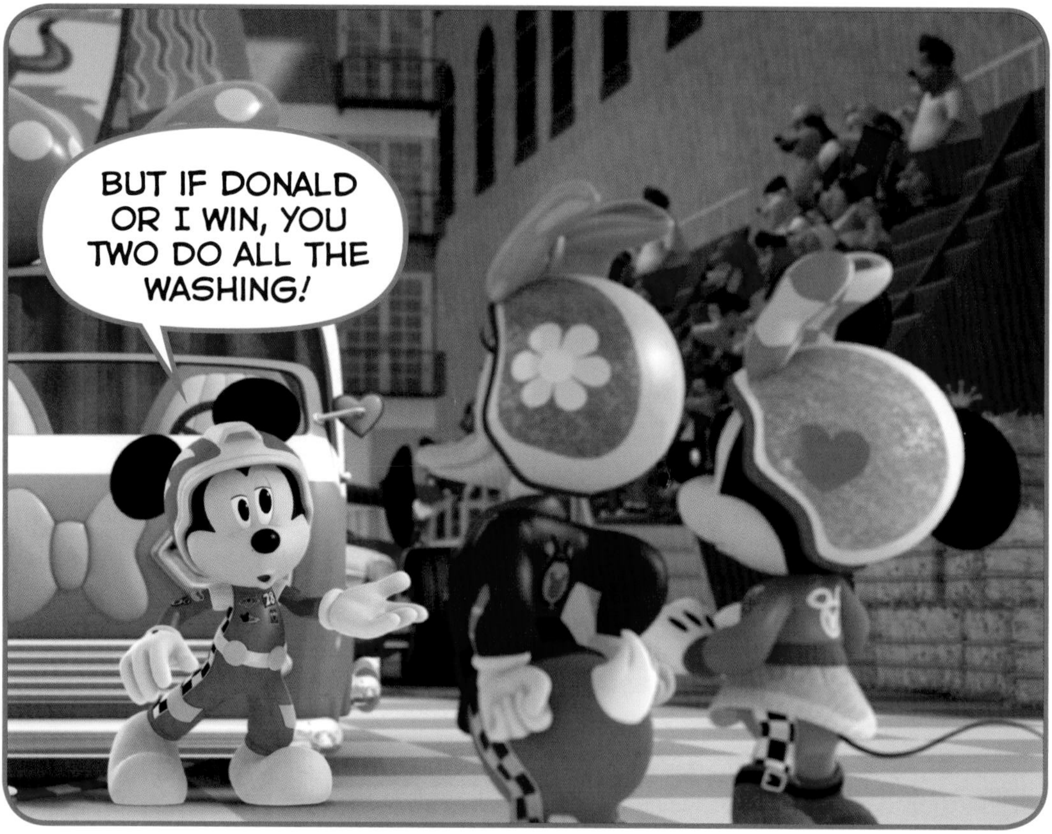
BUT IF DONALD OR I WIN, YOU TWO DO ALL THE WASHING!

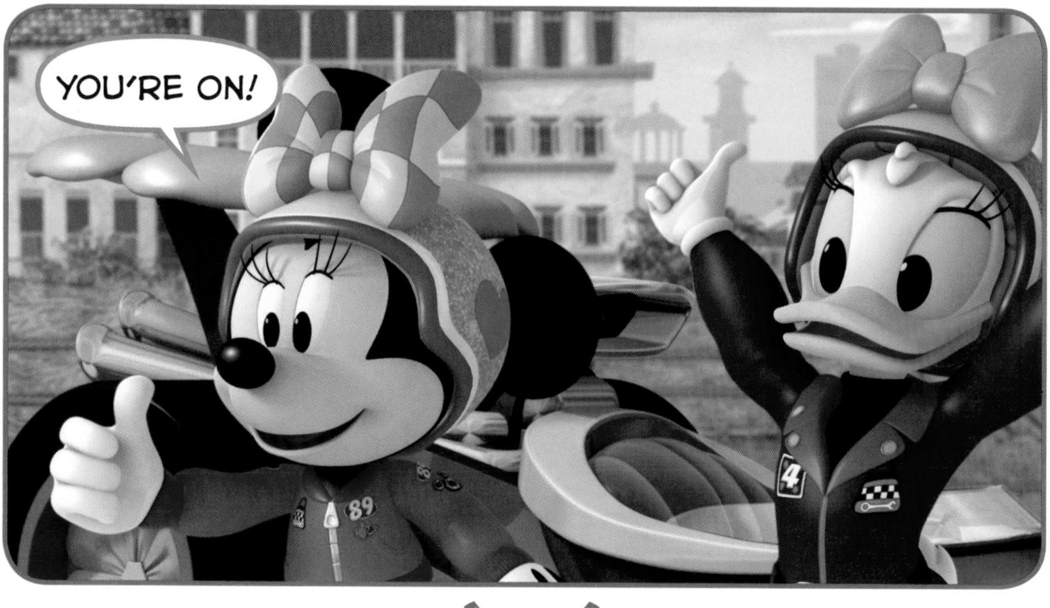
YOU'RE ON!

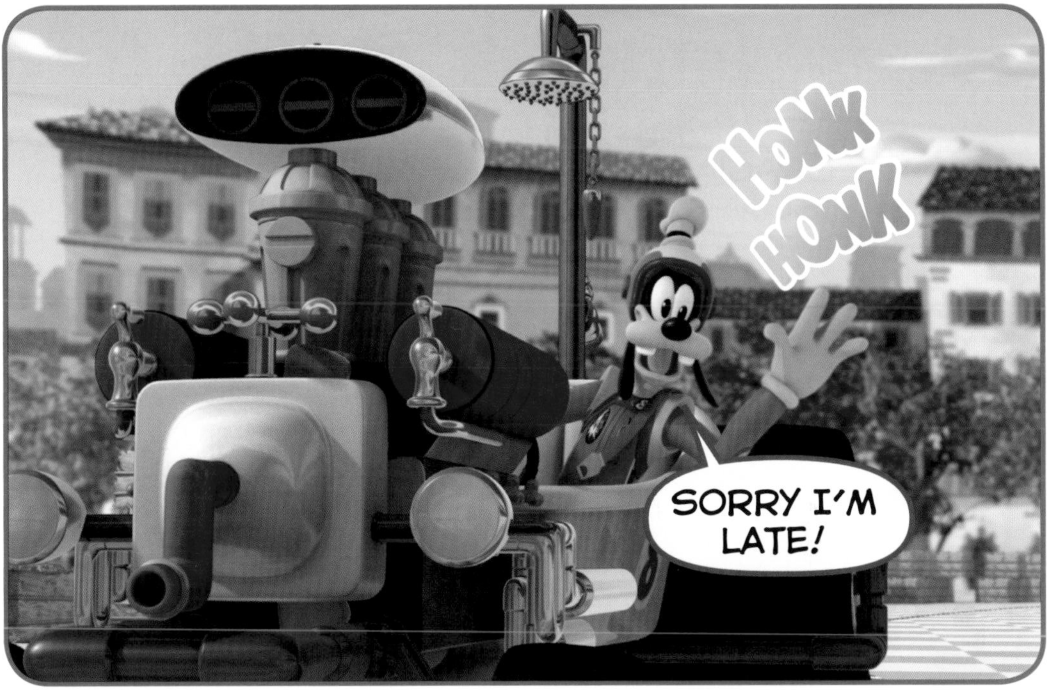
HONK HONK
SORRY I'M LATE!

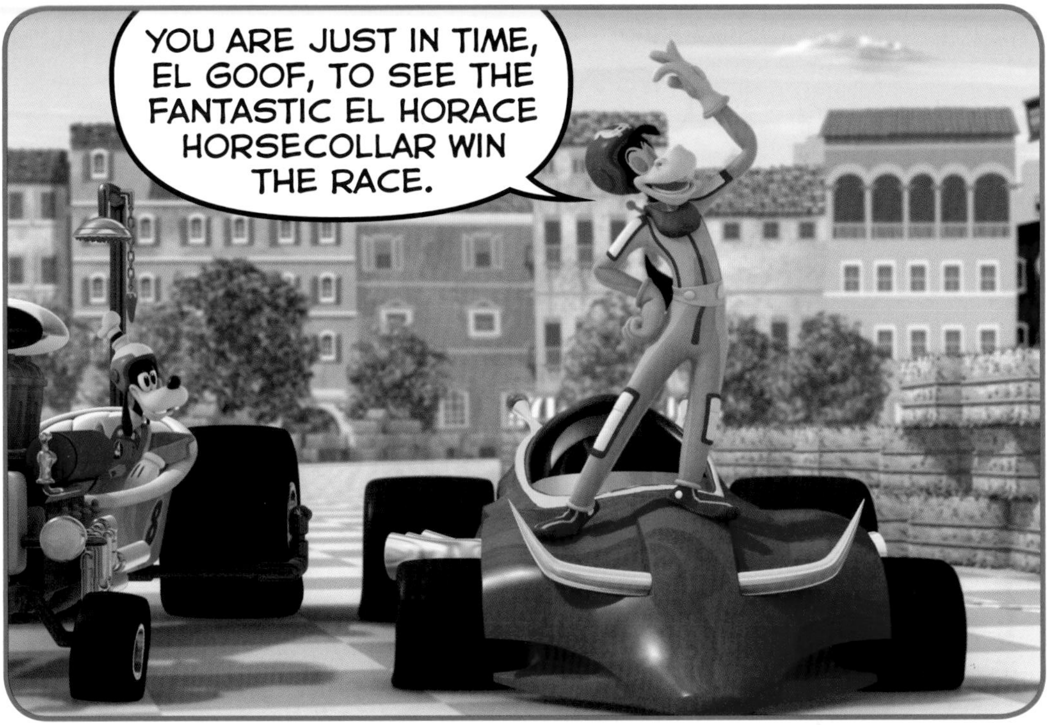
YOU ARE JUST IN TIME, EL GOOF, TO SEE THE FANTASTIC EL HORACE HORSECOLLAR WIN THE RACE.

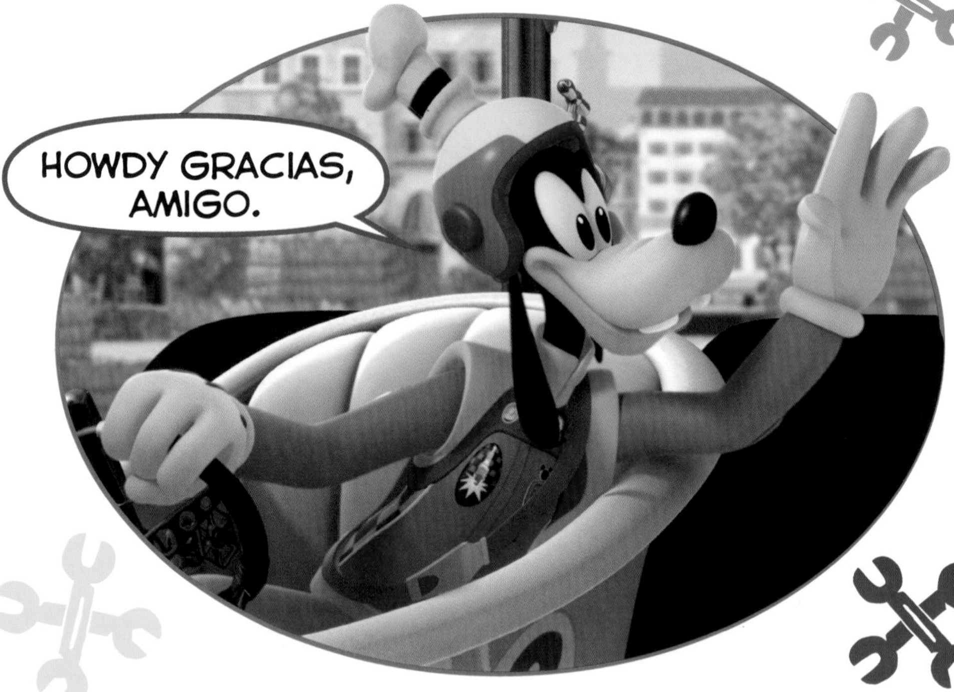
HOWDY GRACIAS, AMIGO.

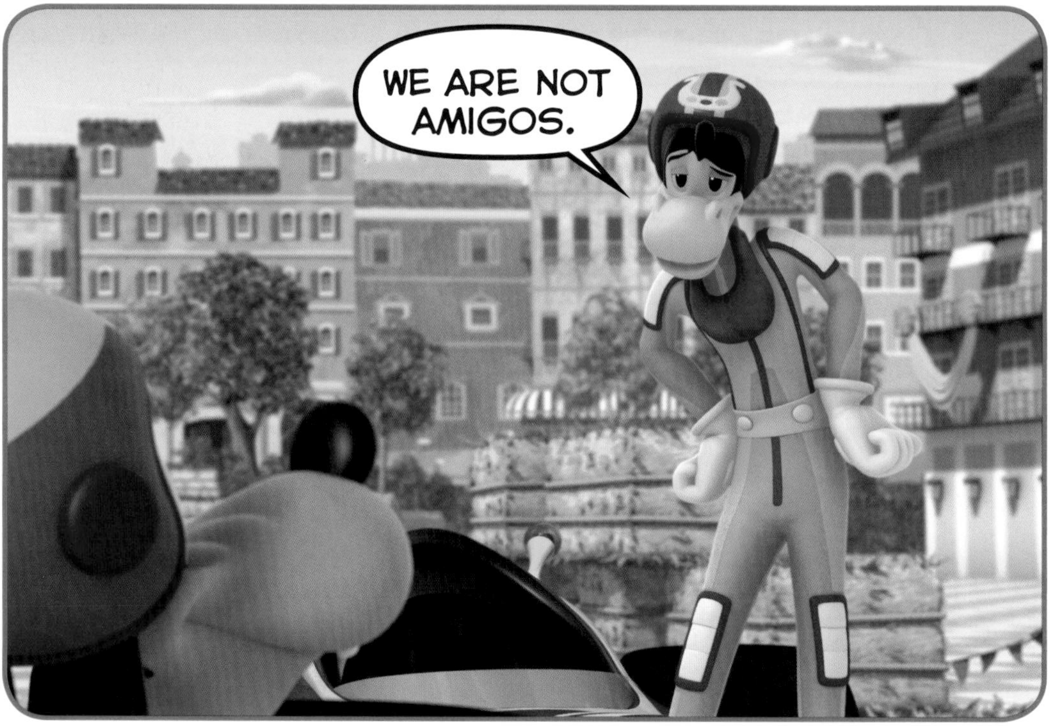
WE ARE NOT AMIGOS.

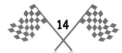

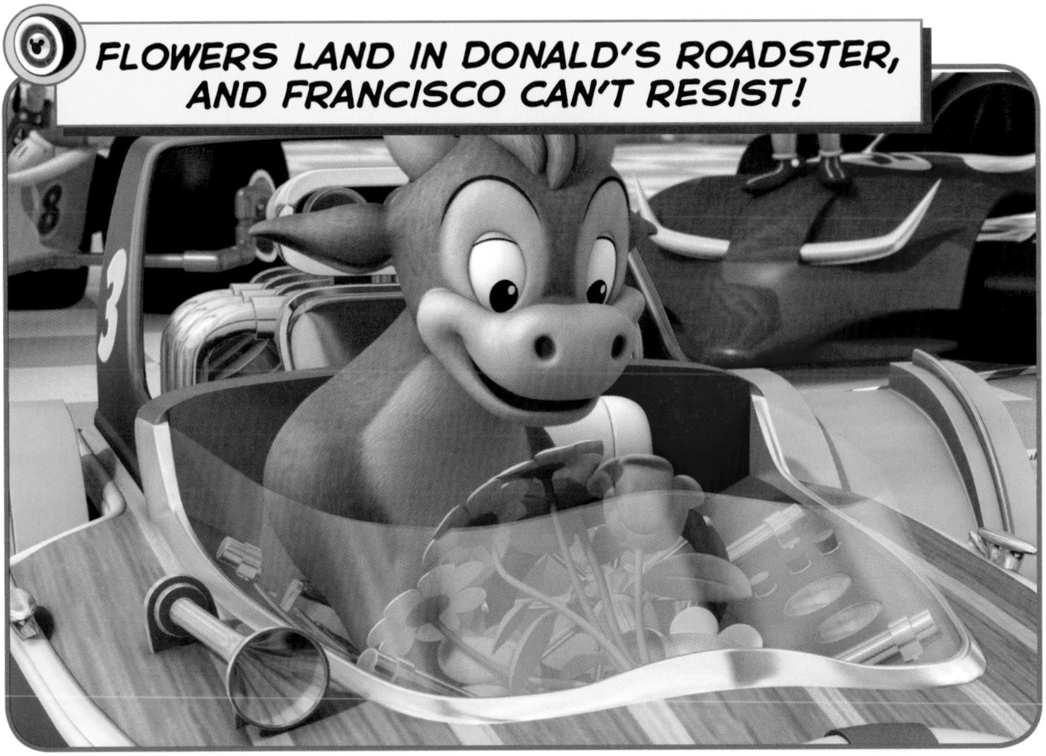
FLOWERS LAND IN DONALD'S ROADSTER, AND FRANCISCO CAN'T RESIST!

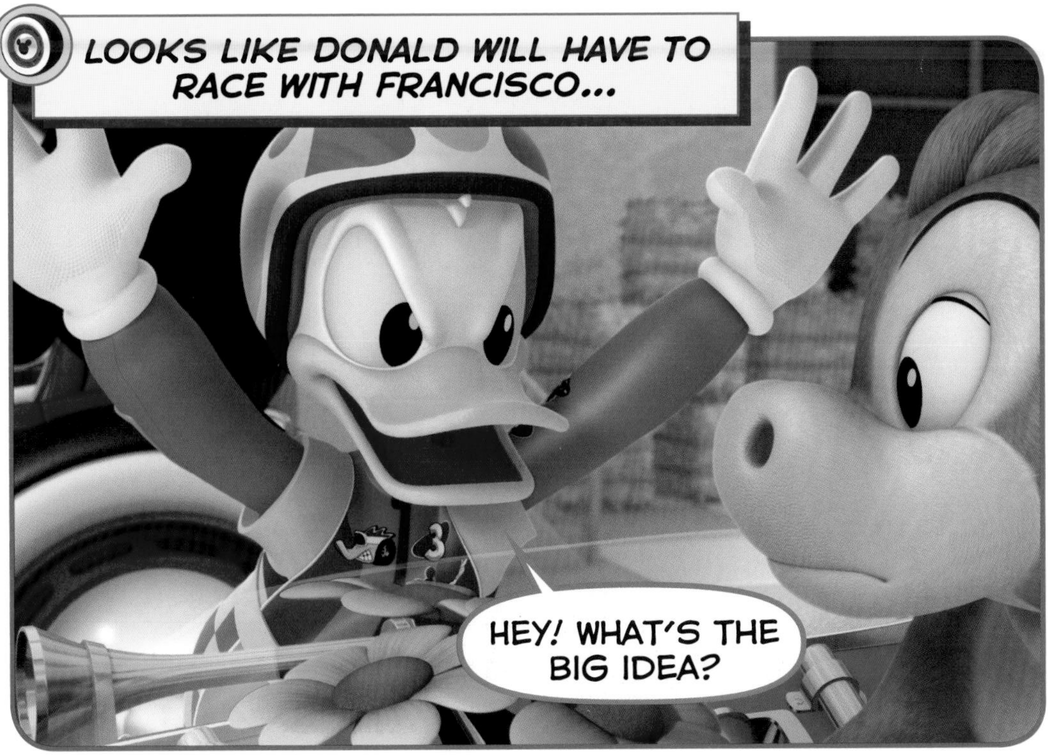
LOOKS LIKE DONALD WILL HAVE TO RACE WITH FRANCISCO...
HEY! WHAT'S THE BIG IDEA?

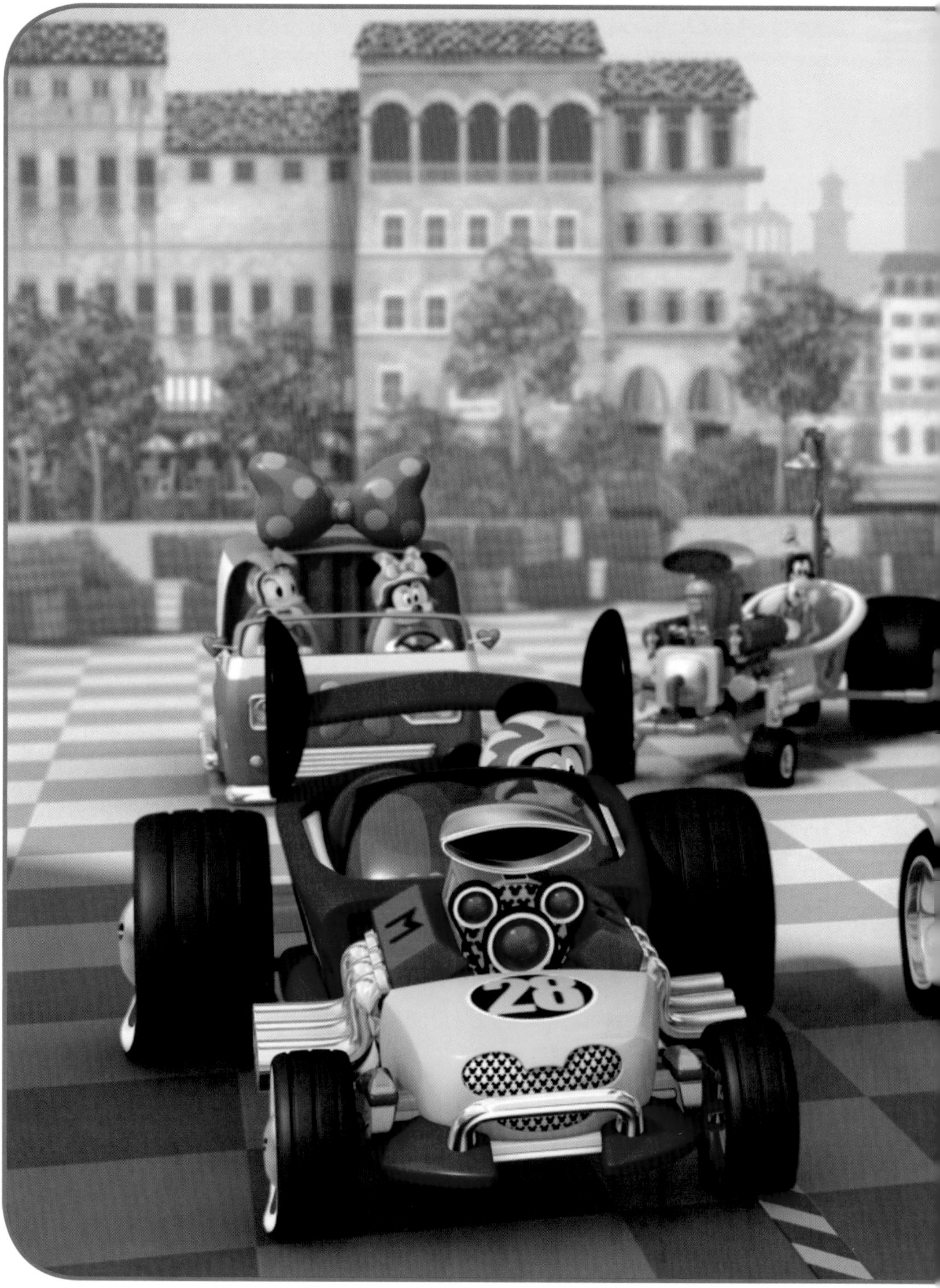
28

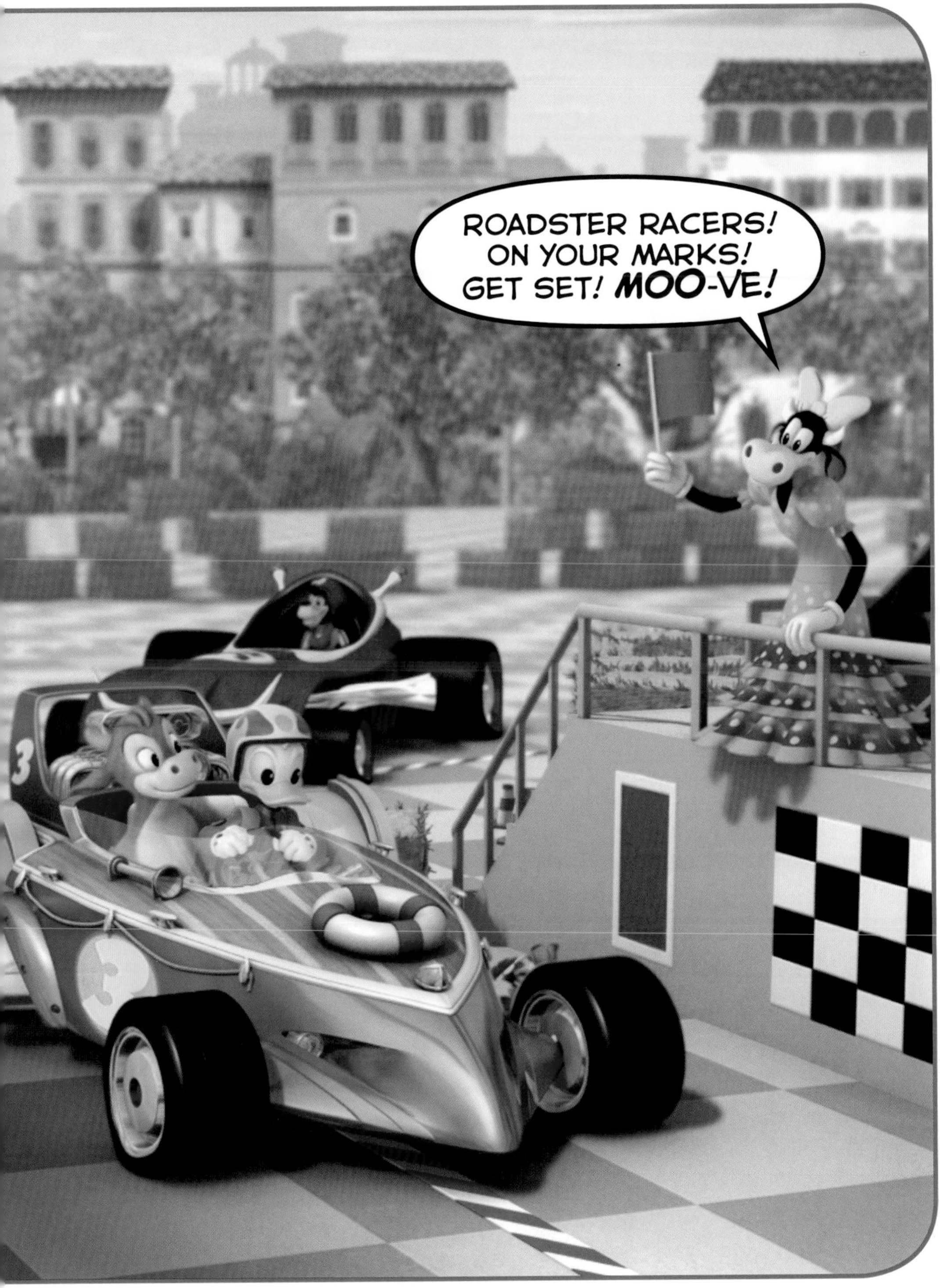
ROADSTER RACERS! ON YOUR MARKS! GET SET! MOO-VE!
3

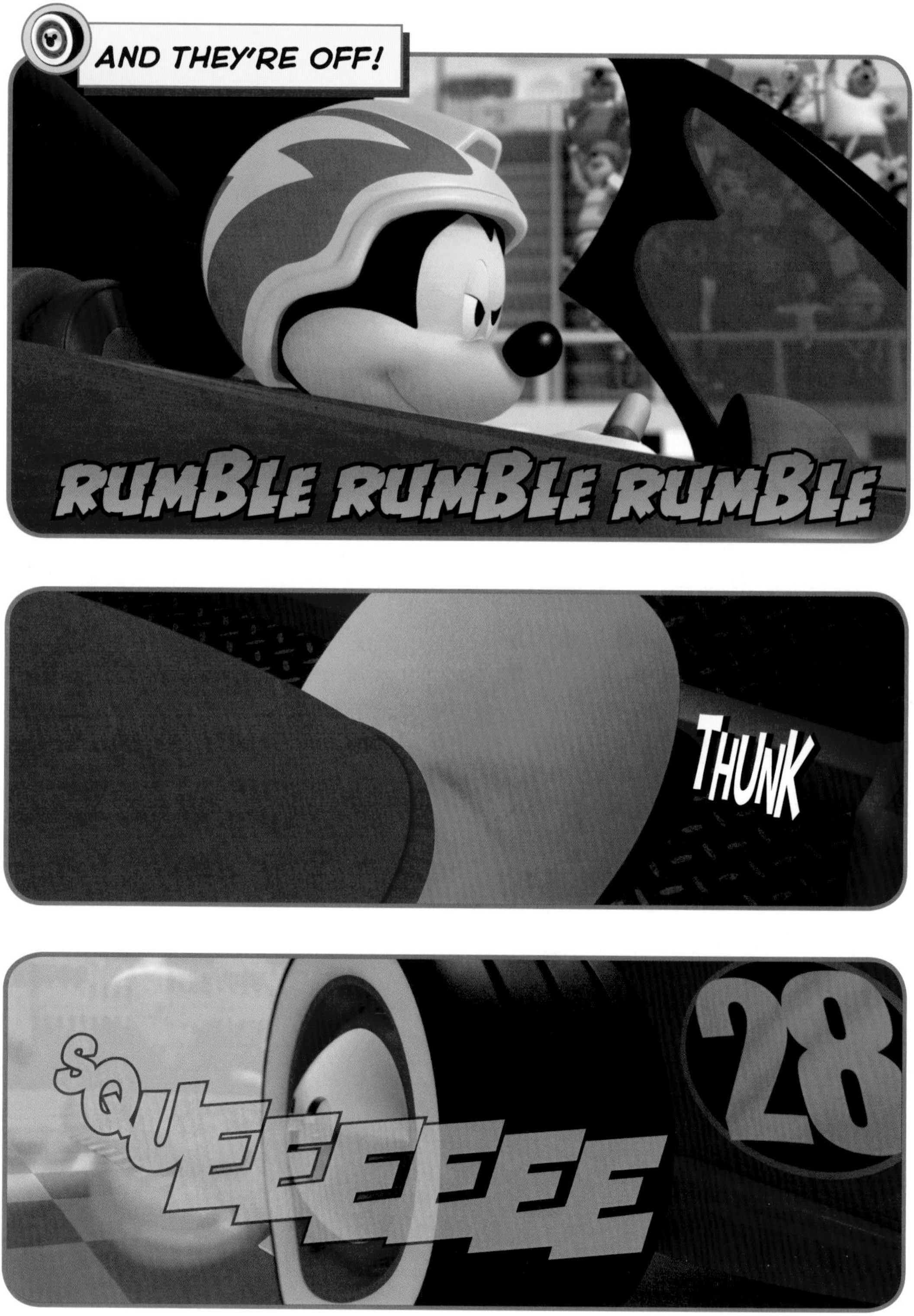
AND THEY'RE OFF!
RUMBLE RUMBLE RUMBLE
THUNK
SQUEEEEEE
28

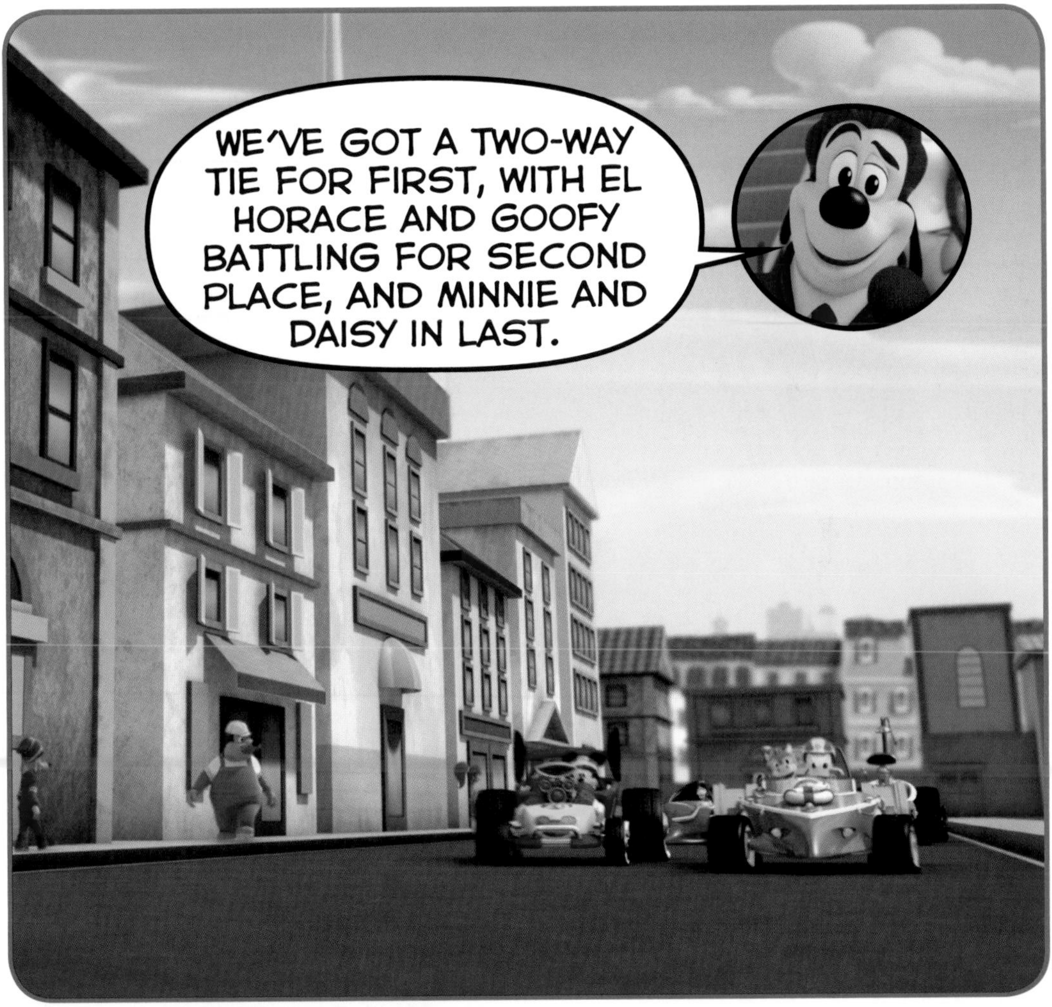
WE'VE GOT A TWO-WAY TIE FOR FIRST, WITH EL HORACE AND GOOFY BATTLING FOR SECOND PLACE, AND MINNIE AND DAISY IN LAST.

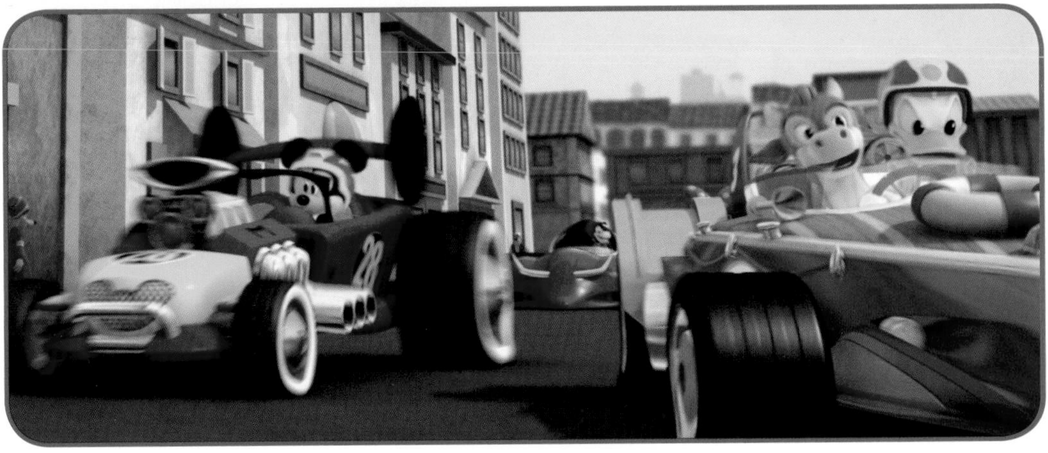

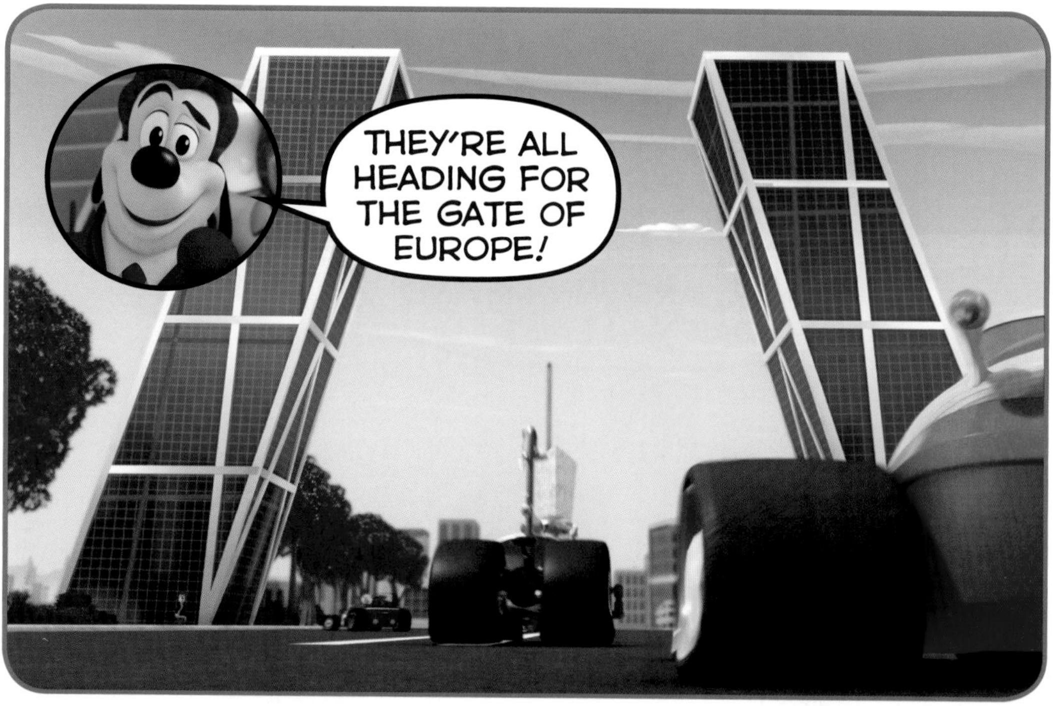
THEY'RE ALL HEADING FOR THE GATE OF EUROPE!

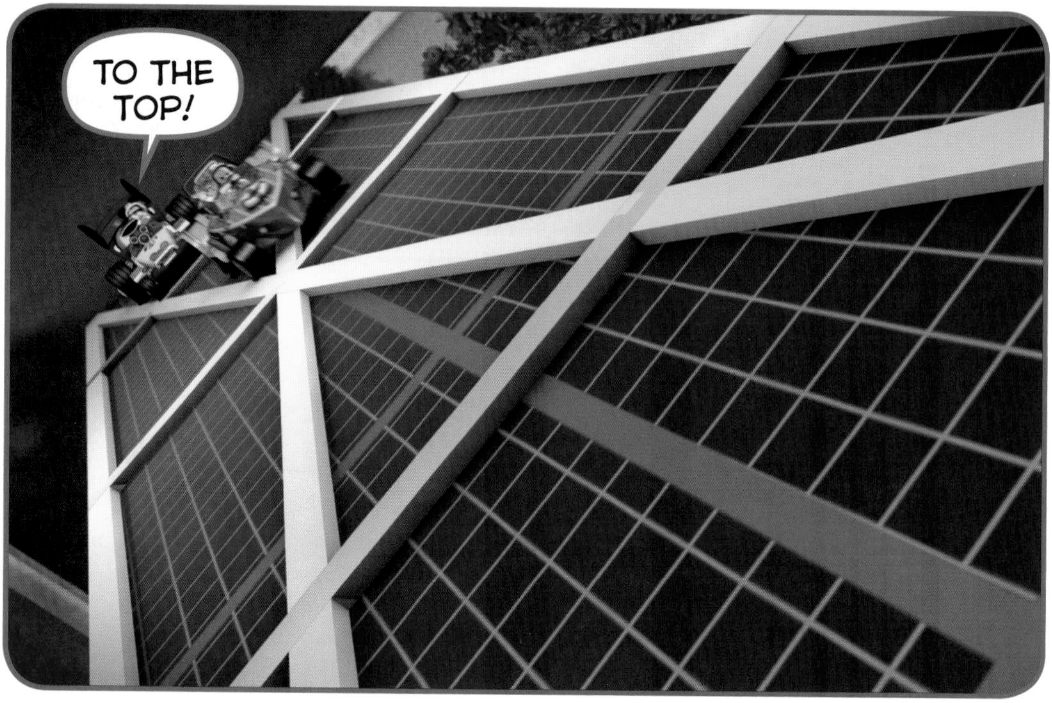
TO THE TOP!

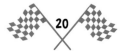

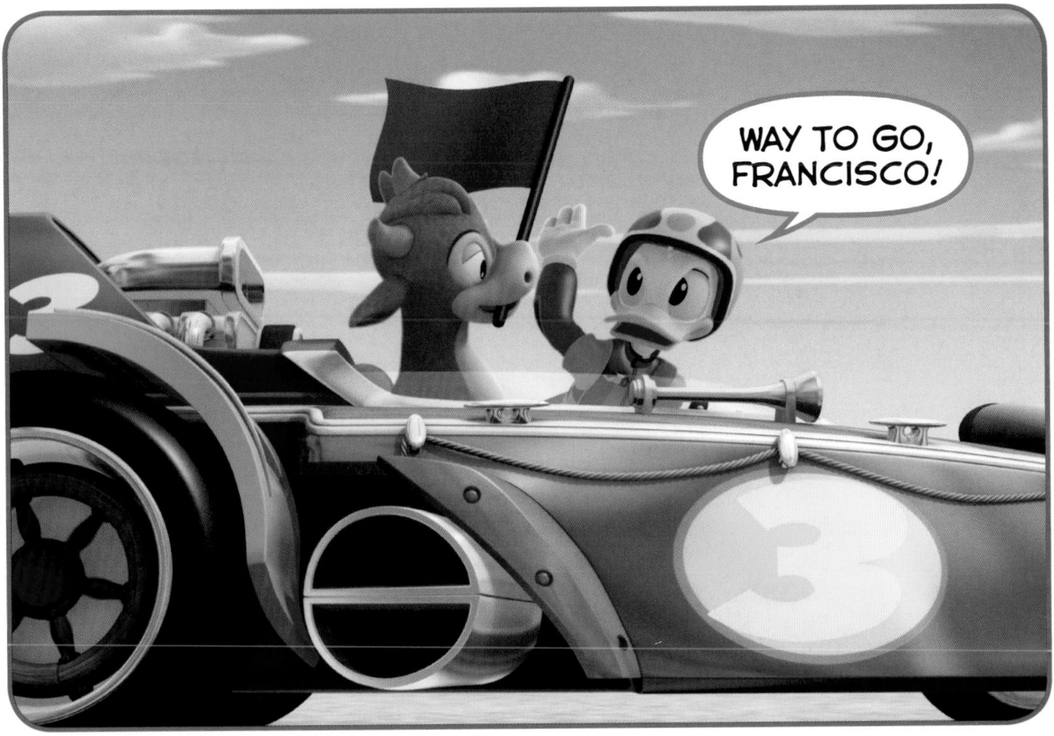
WAY TO GO, FRANCISCO!

DONALD AND MICKEY HAVE THEIR FIRST FLAGS, BUT MINNIE AND DAISY AREN'T EVEN AT THE GATE!

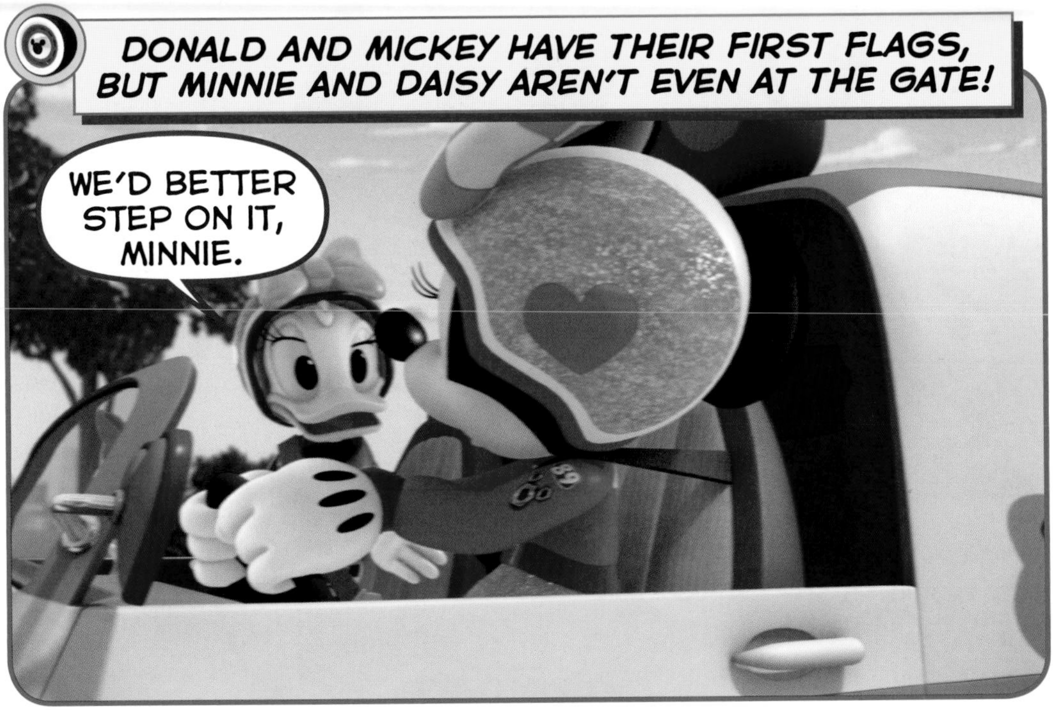
WE'D BETTER STEP ON IT, MINNIE.

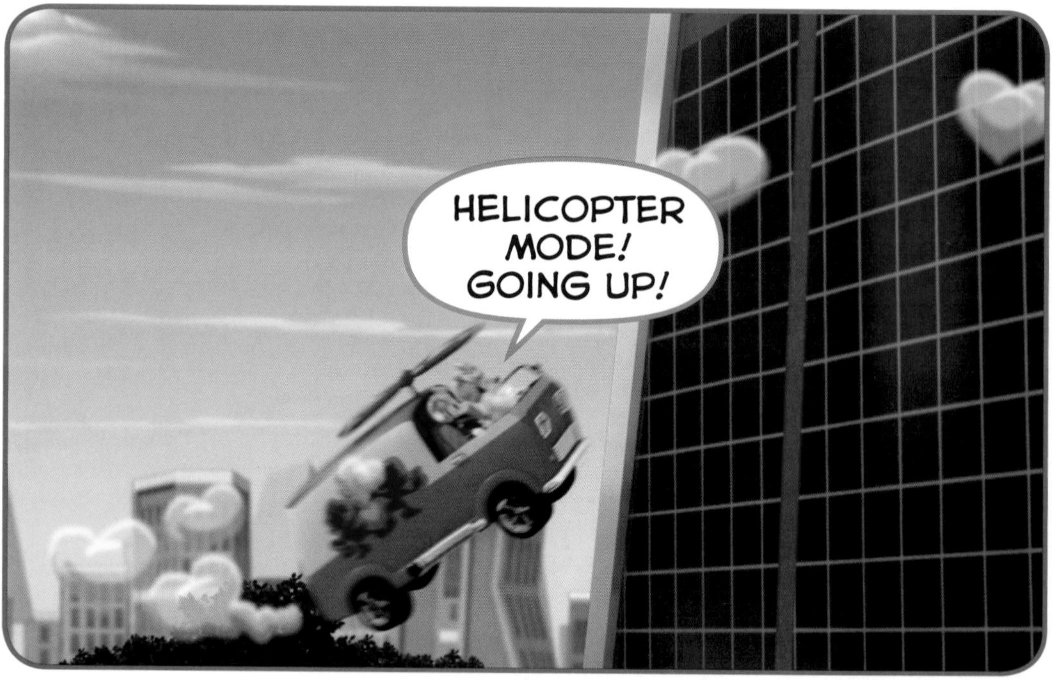
HELICOPTER MODE! GOING UP!

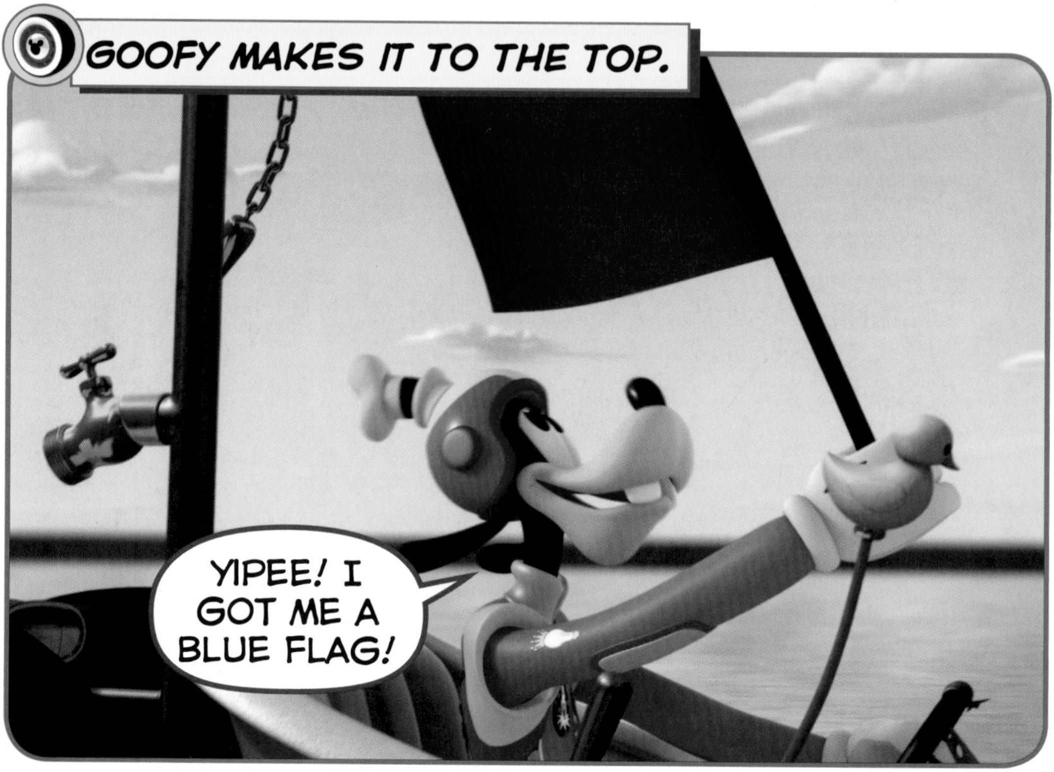
GOOFY MAKES IT TO THE TOP.
YIPEE! I GOT ME A BLUE FLAG!

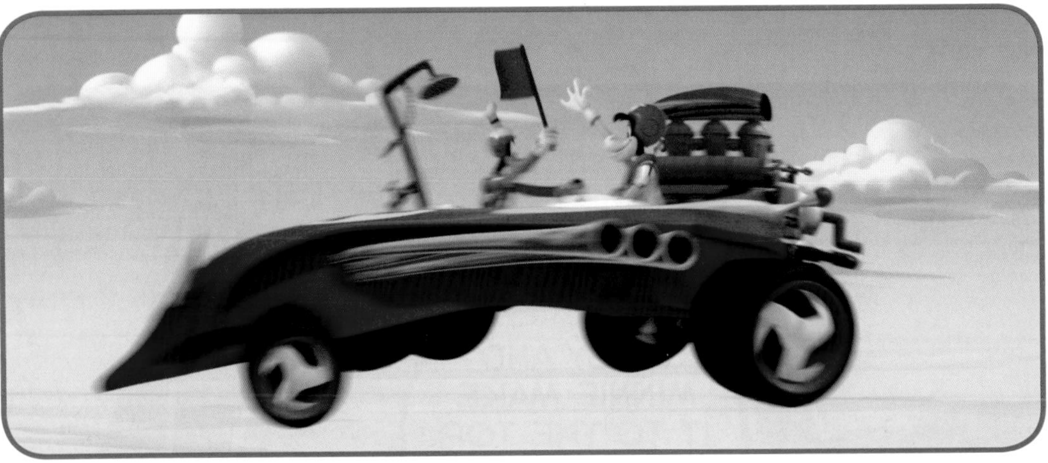

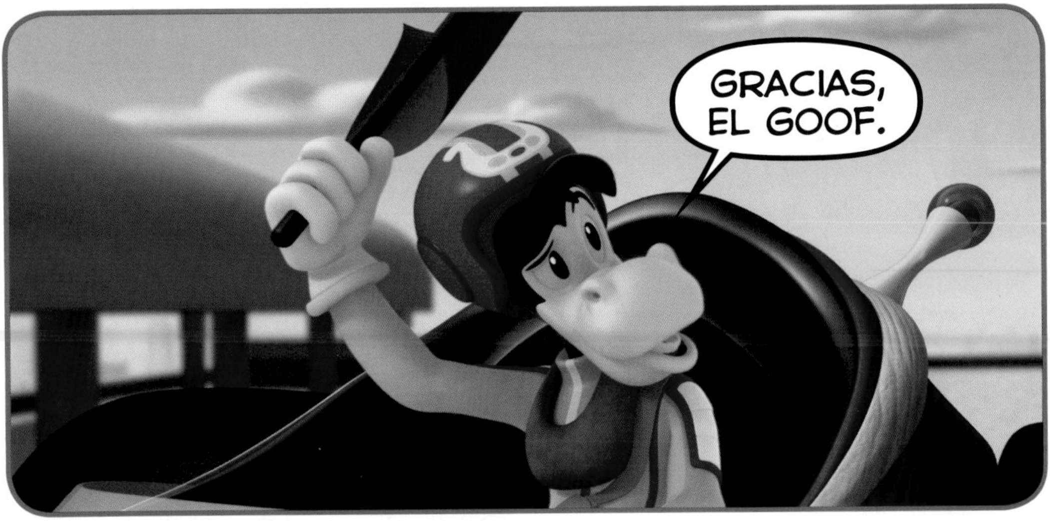
GRACIAS, EL GOOF.

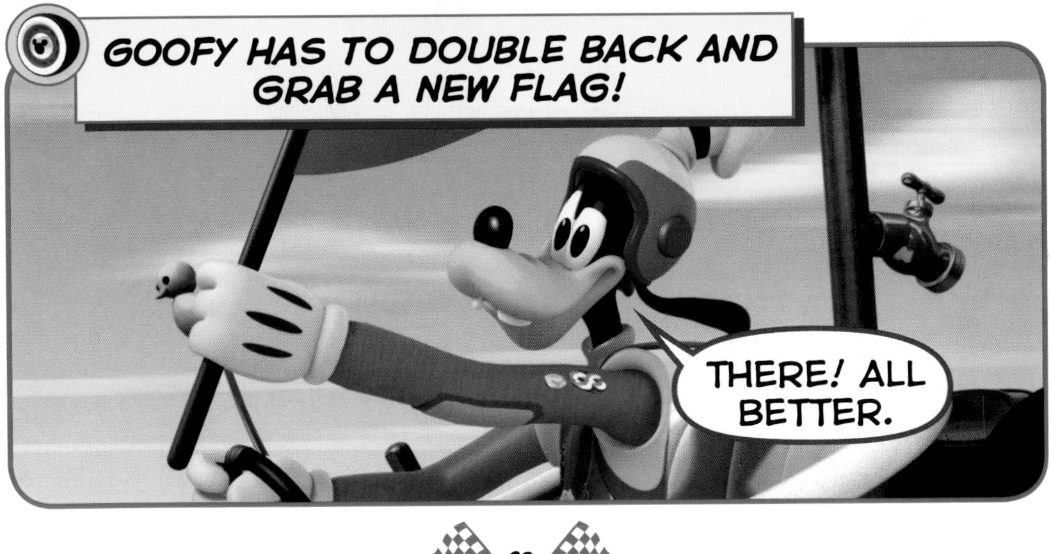
GOOFY HAS TO DOUBLE BACK AND GRAB A NEW FLAG!
THERE! ALL BETTER.

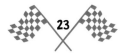

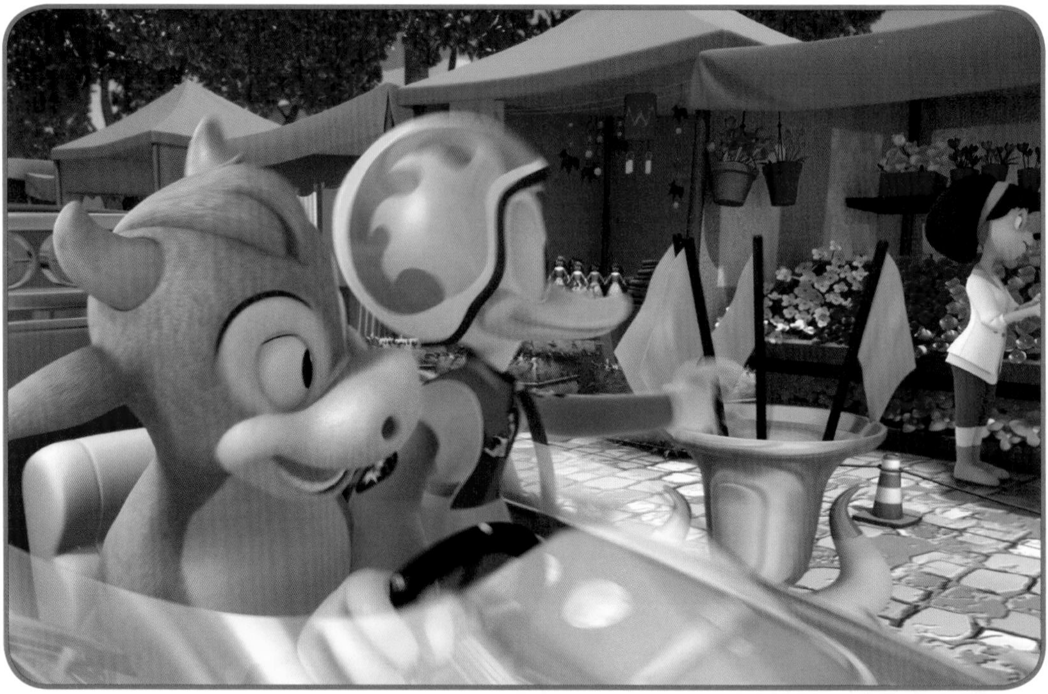

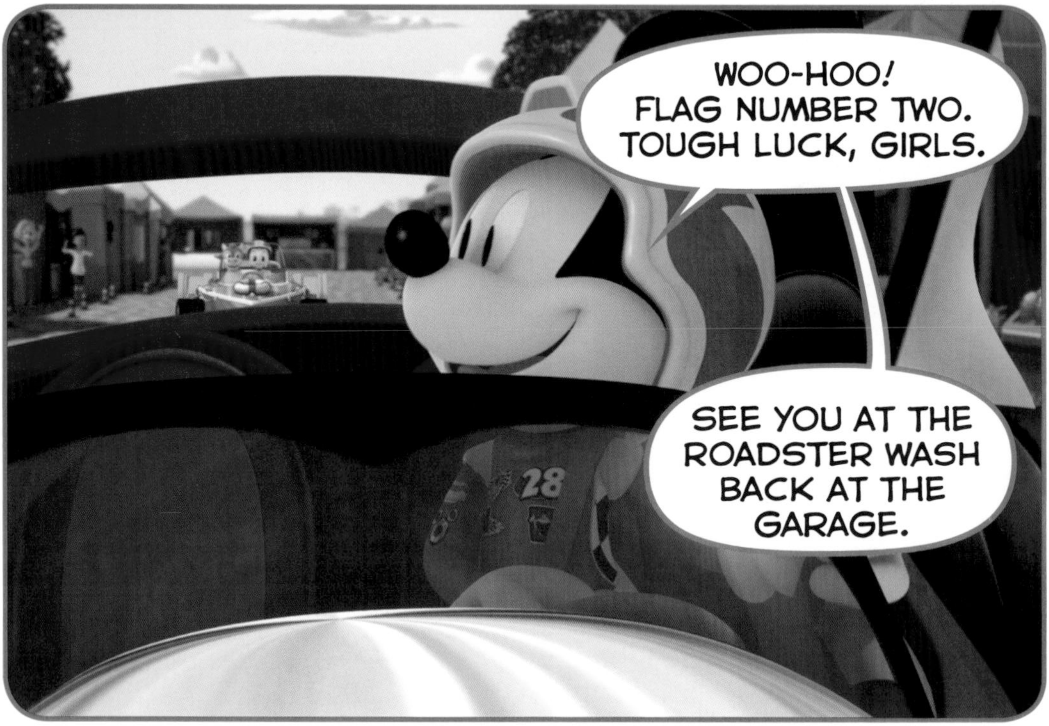
WOO-HOO!
FLAG NUMBER TWO.
TOUGH LUCK, GIRLS.
SEE YOU AT THE ROADSTER WASH BACK AT THE GARAGE.

EL HORACE BUMPS INTO GOOFY.

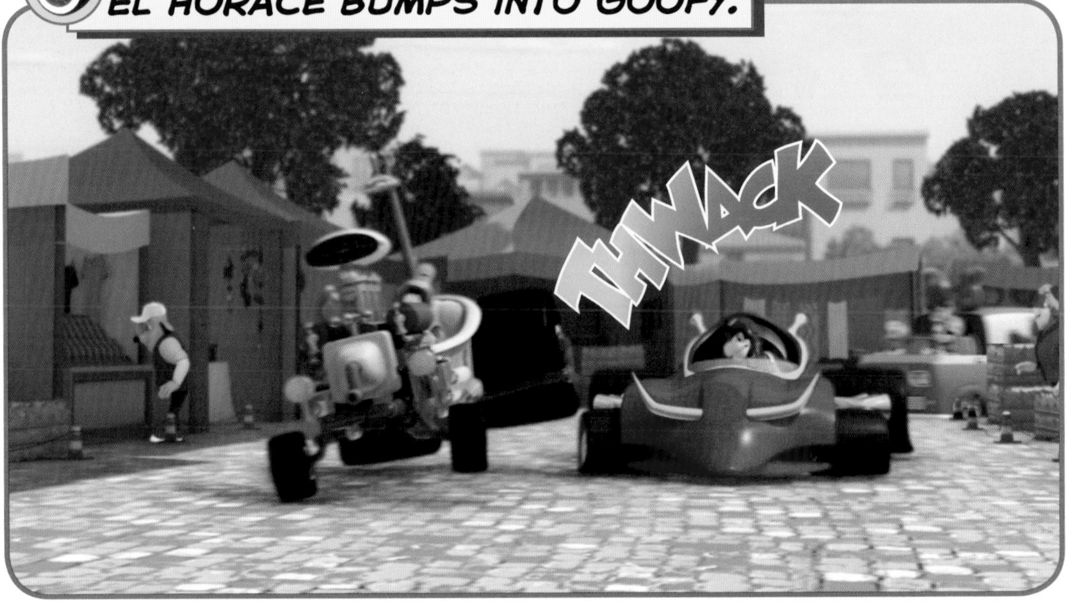
THWACK

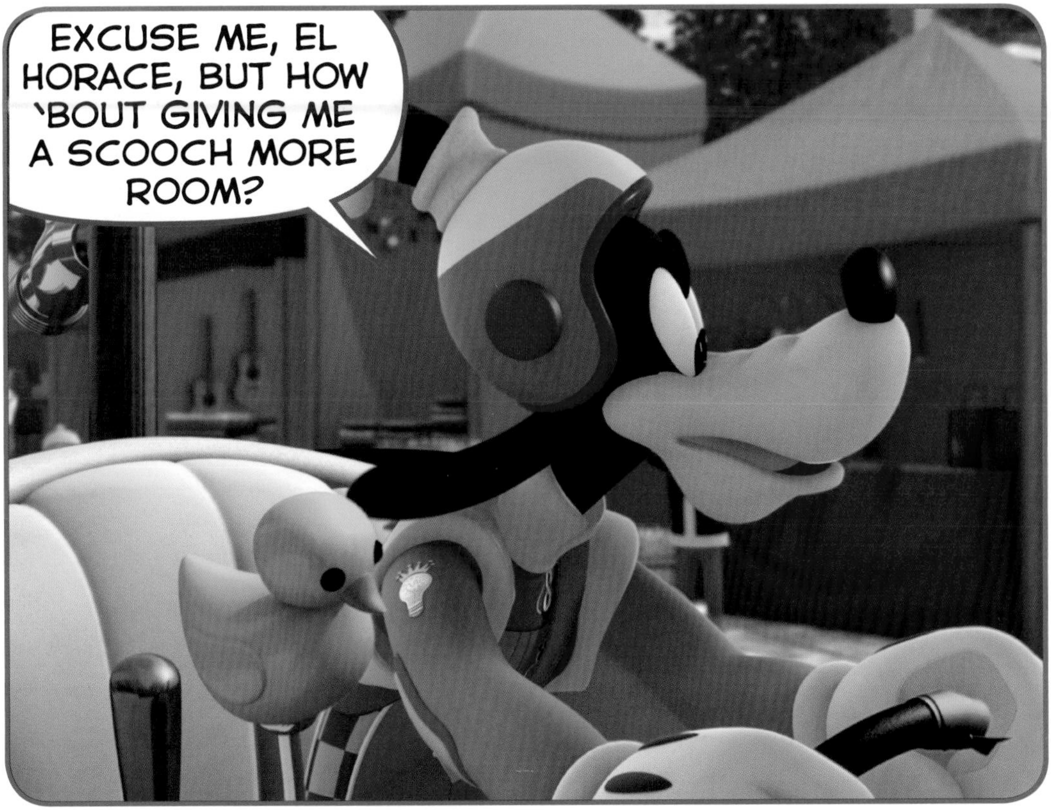
EXCUSE ME, EL HORACE, BUT HOW 'BOUT GIVING ME A SCOOCH MORE ROOM?

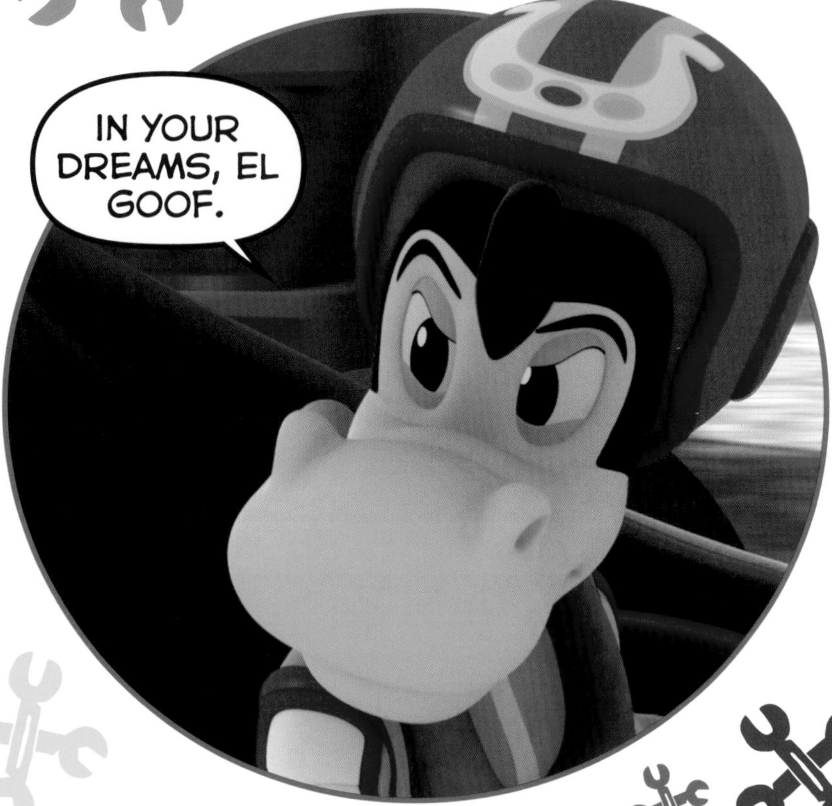
IN YOUR DREAMS, EL GOOF.

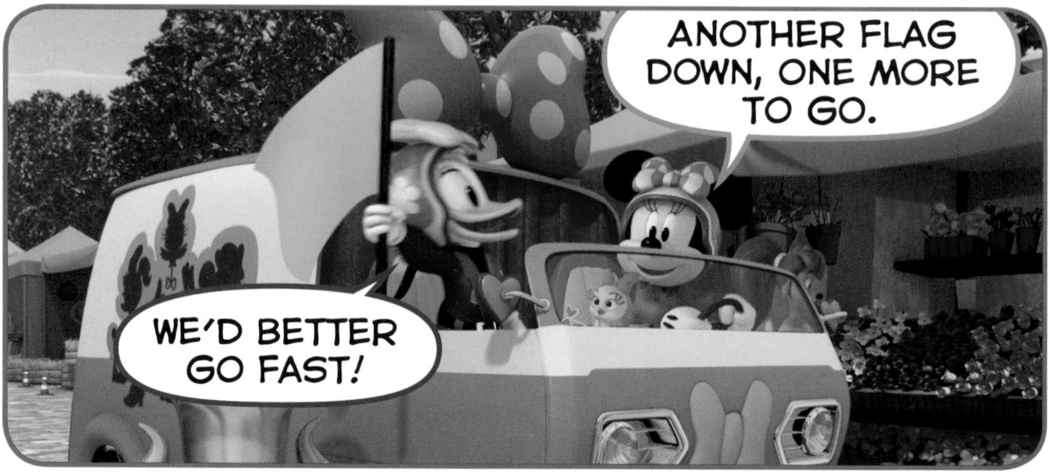
ANOTHER FLAG DOWN, ONE MORE TO GO.
WE'D BETTER GO FAST!

MICKEY AND DONALD RACE AHEAD TO THE LAST FLAG AT LAS VENTAS ARENA!

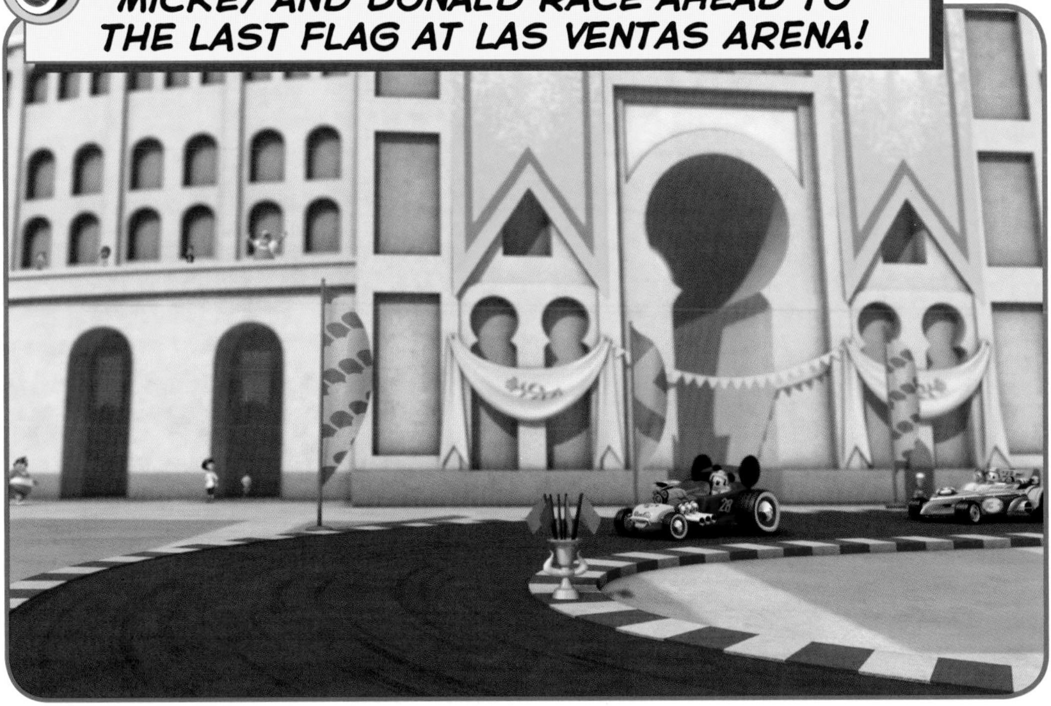

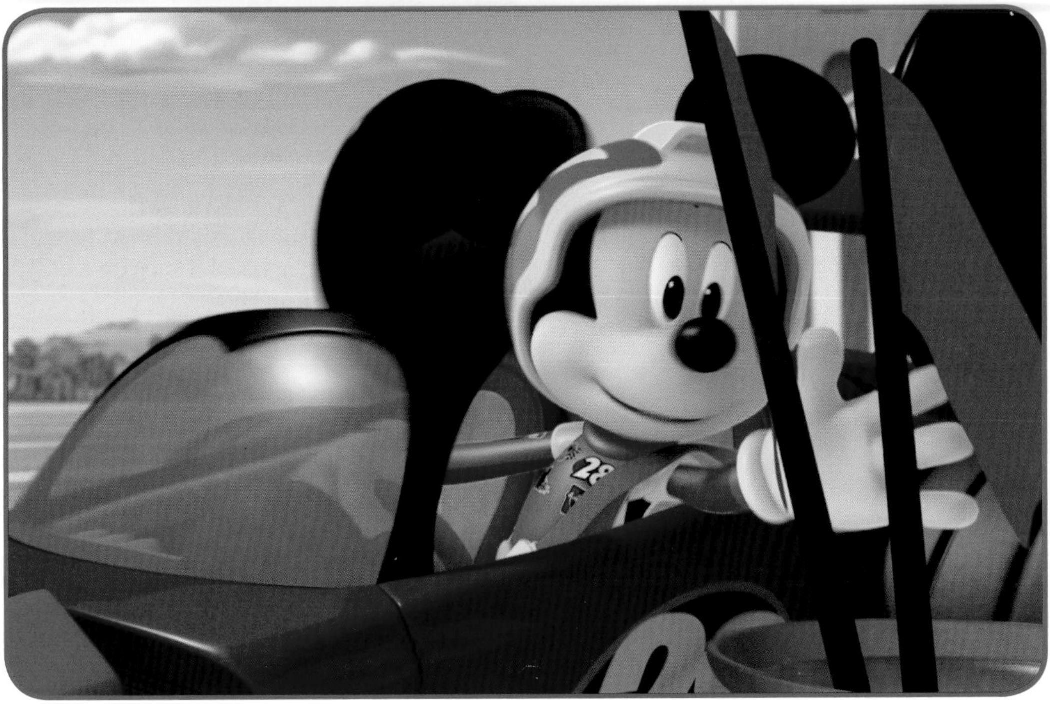

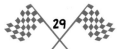

NOW LET'S FINISH THIS RACE!

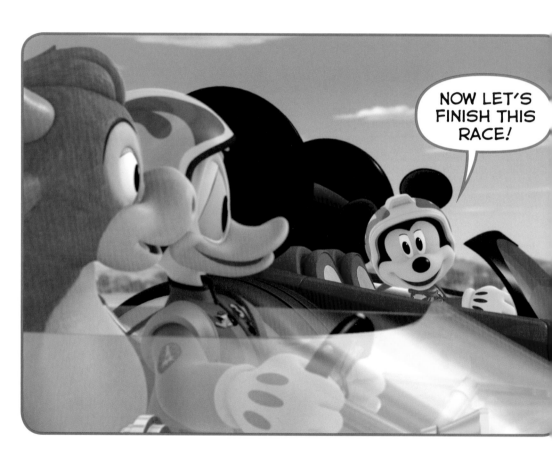

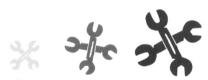

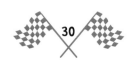

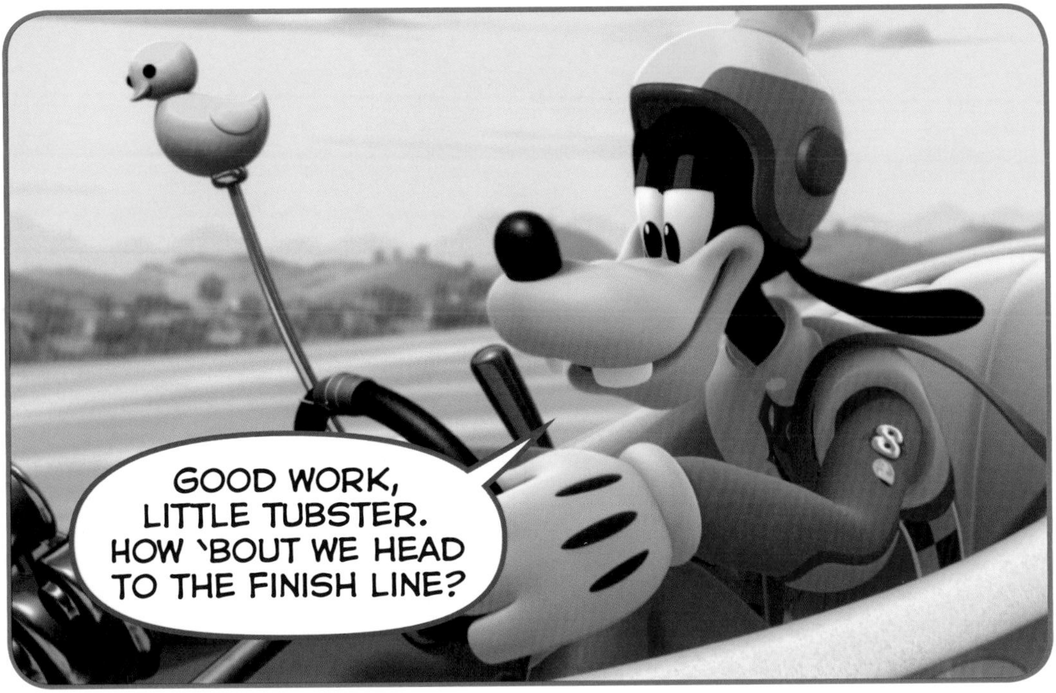
GOOD WORK, LITTLE TUBSTER. HOW 'BOUT WE HEAD TO THE FINISH LINE?

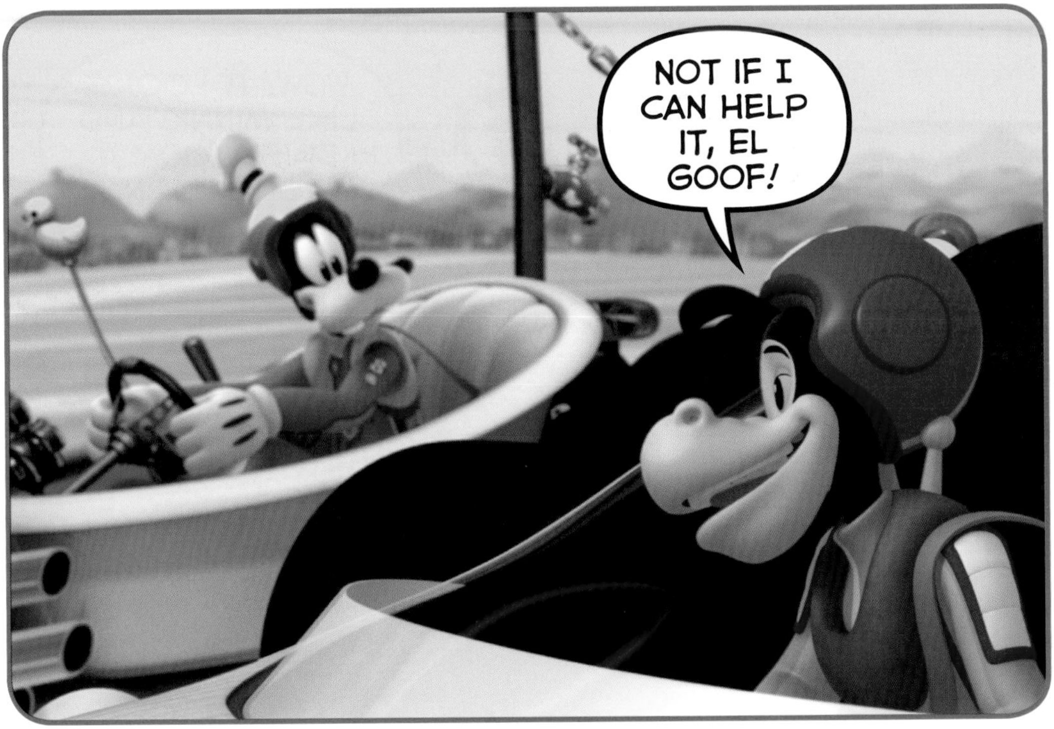
NOT IF I CAN HELP IT, EL GOOF!

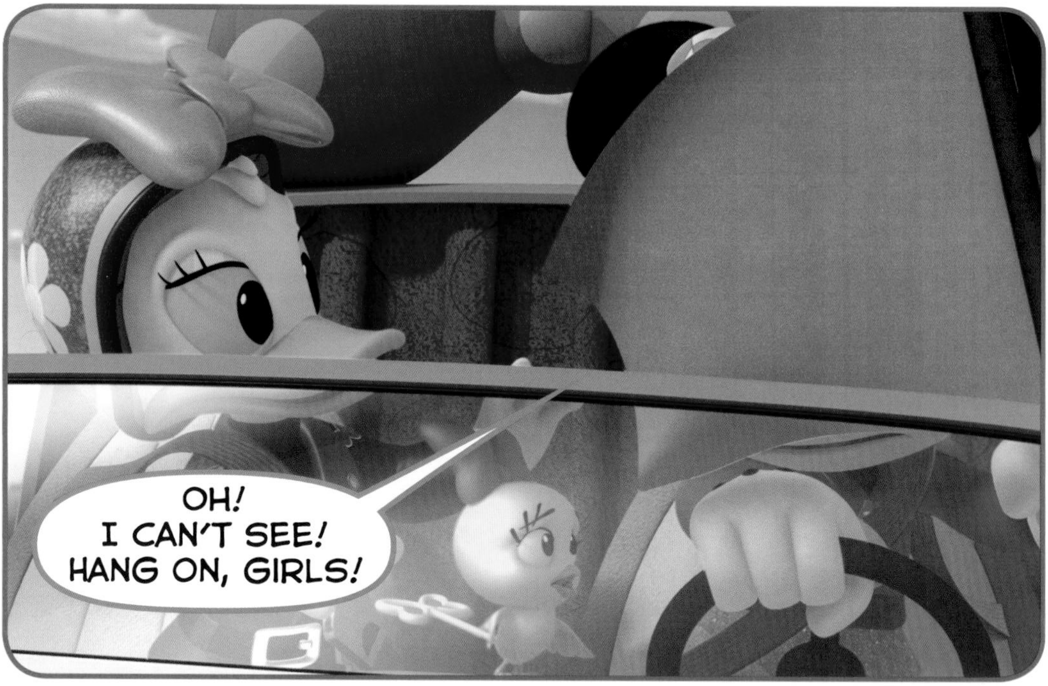
OH!
I CAN'T SEE!
HANG ON, GIRLS!

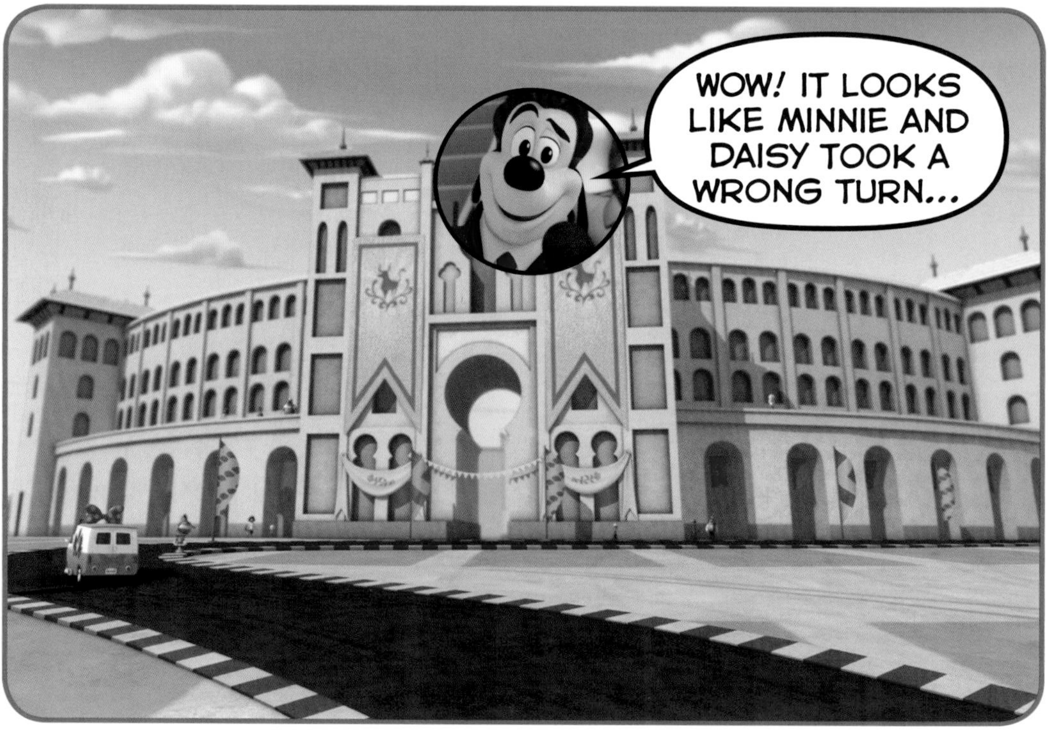
WOW! IT LOOKS
LIKE MINNIE AND
DAISY TOOK A
WRONG TURN...

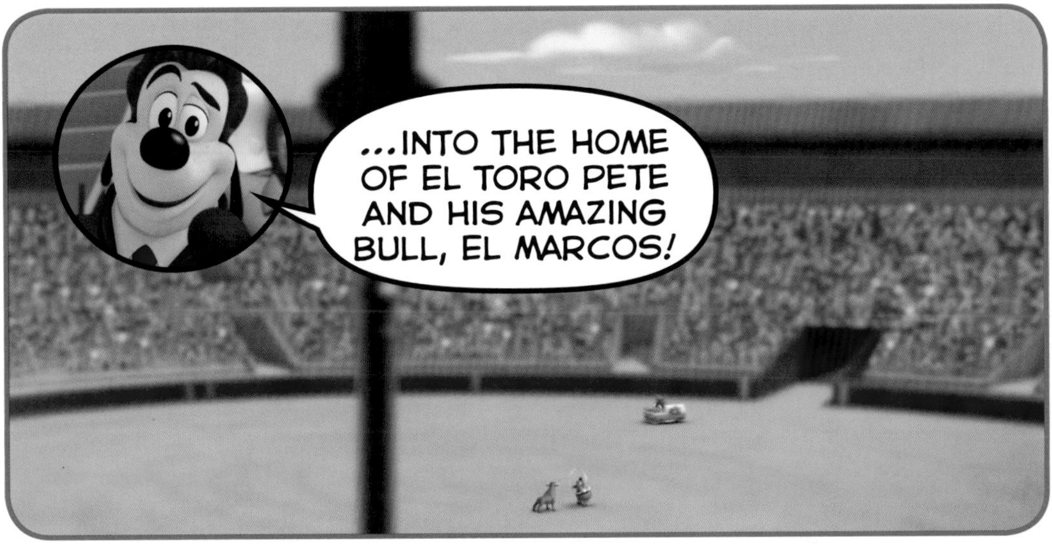
...INTO THE HOME OF EL TORO PETE AND HIS AMAZING BULL, EL MARCOS!

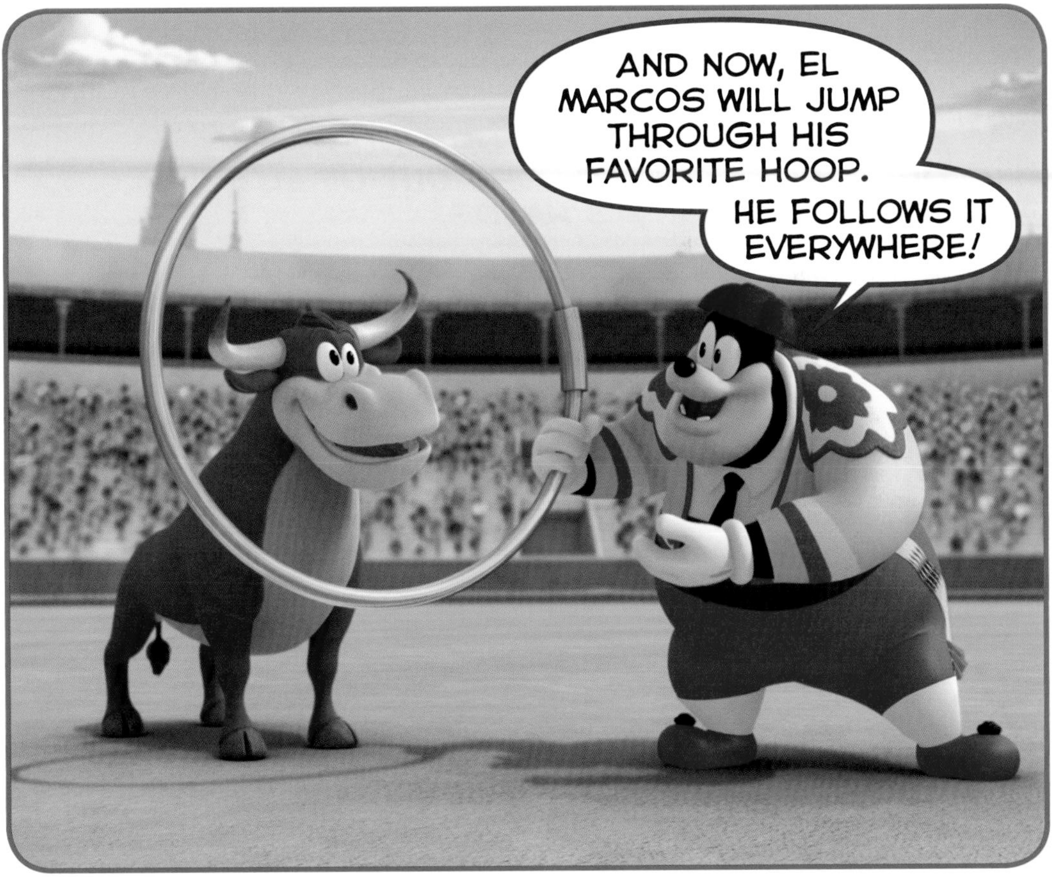
AND NOW, EL MARCOS WILL JUMP THROUGH HIS FAVORITE HOOP.
HE FOLLOWS IT EVERYWHERE!

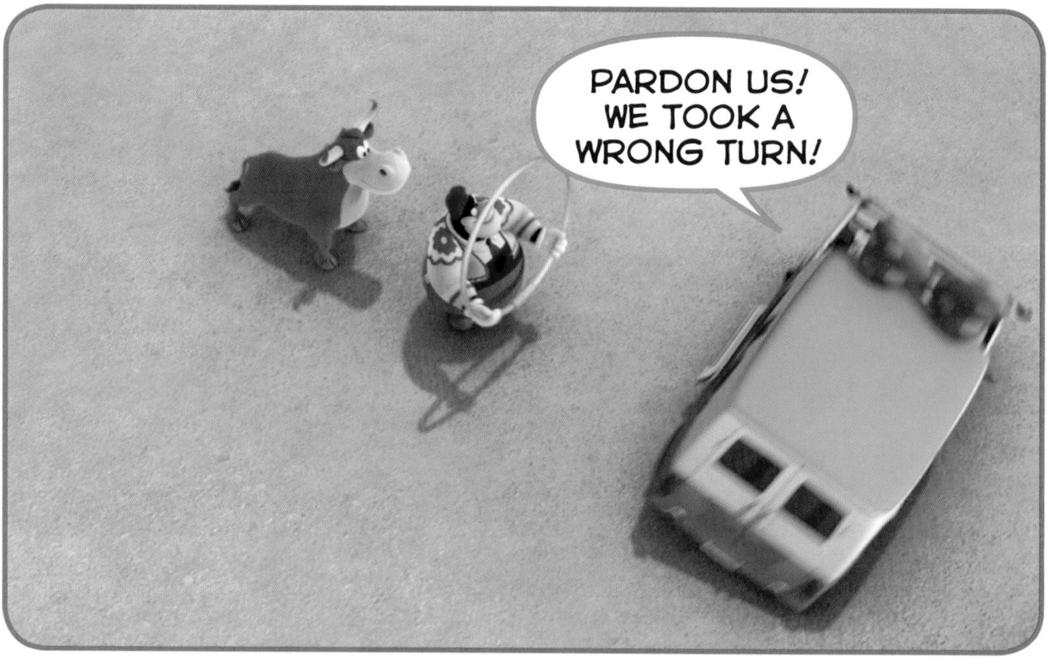
PARDON US! WE TOOK A WRONG TURN!

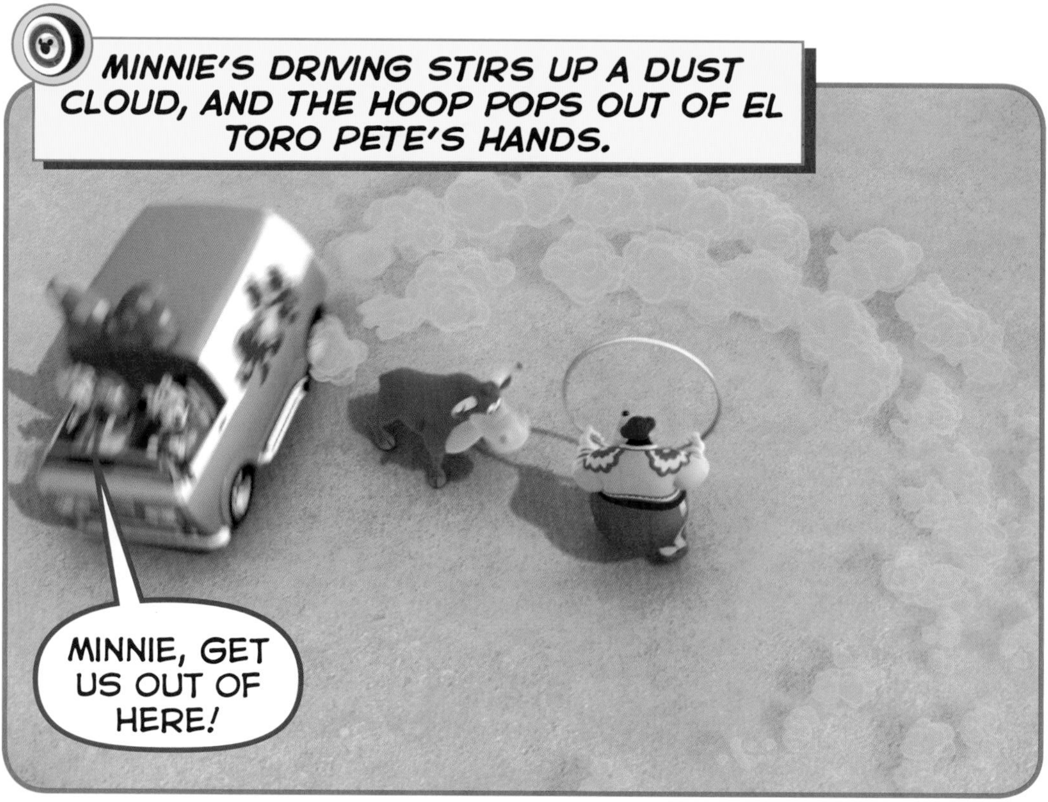
MINNIE'S DRIVING STIRS UP A DUST CLOUD, AND THE HOOP POPS OUT OF EL TORO PETE'S HANDS.
MINNIE, GET US OUT OF HERE!

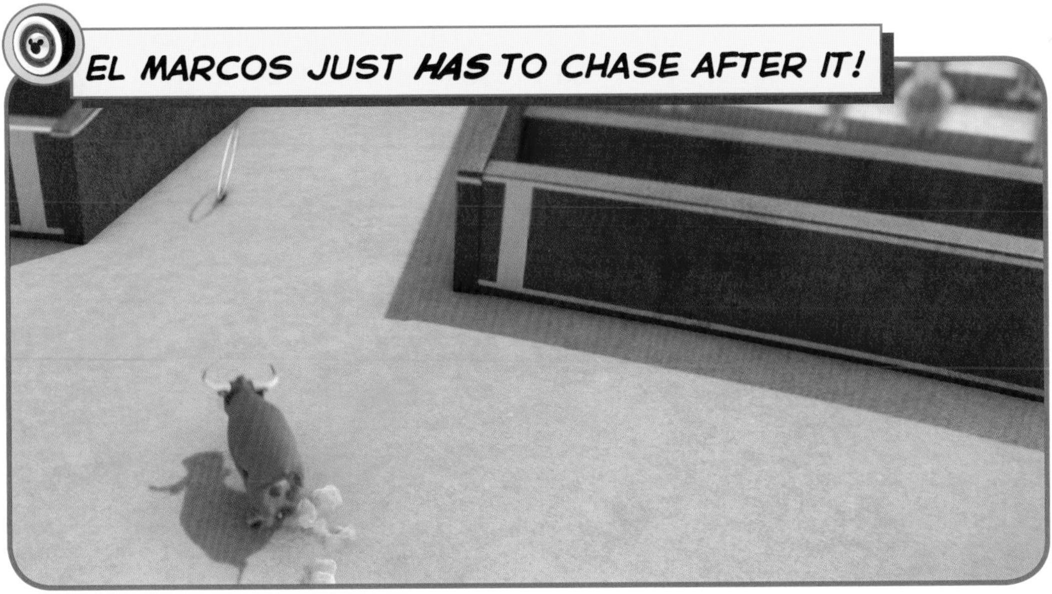
EL MARCOS JUST HAS TO CHASE AFTER IT!

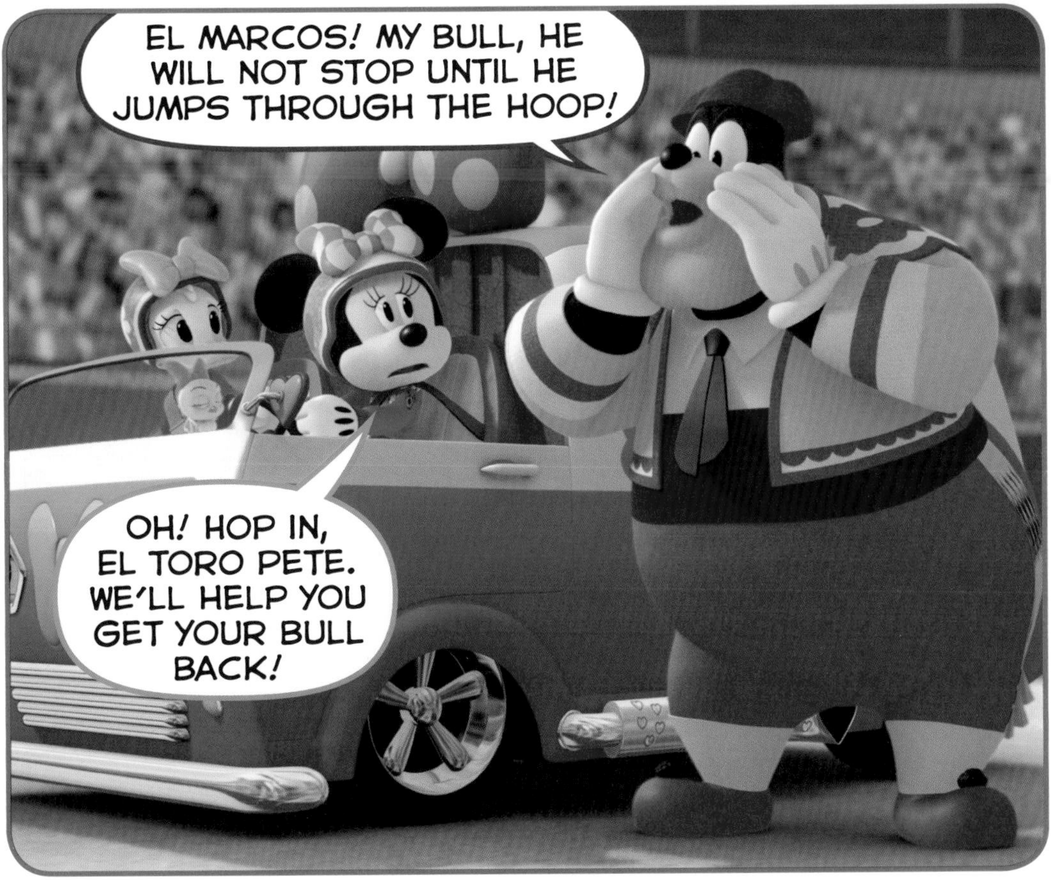
EL MARCOS! MY BULL, HE WILL NOT STOP UNTIL HE JUMPS THROUGH THE HOOP!
OH! HOP IN, EL TORO PETE. WE'LL HELP YOU GET YOUR BULL BACK!

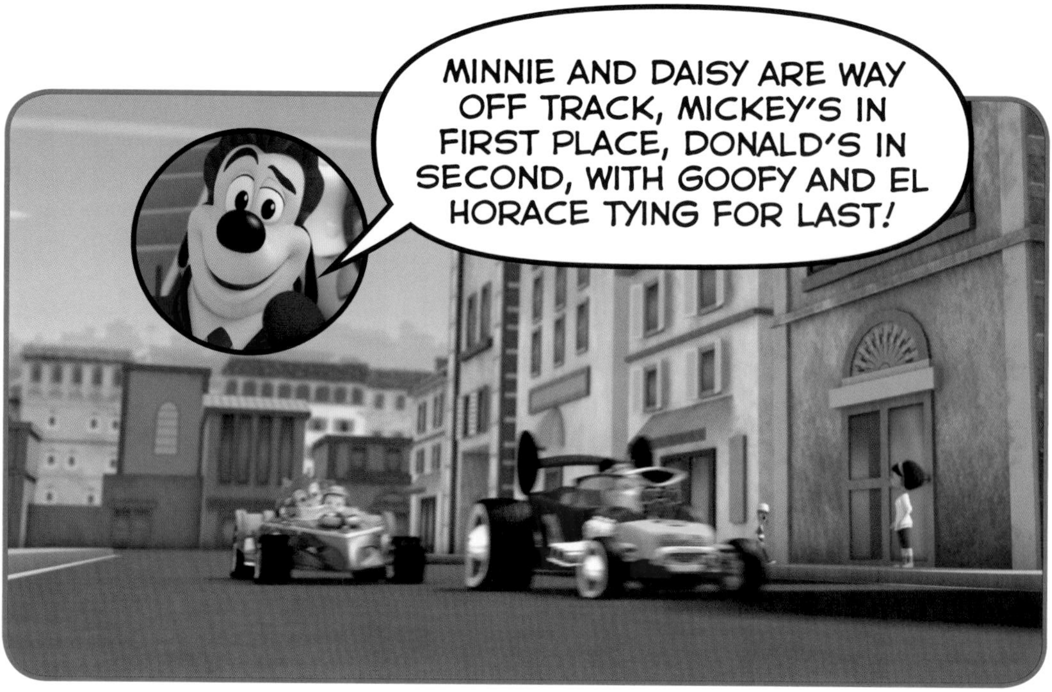
MINNIE AND DAISY ARE WAY OFF TRACK, MICKEY'S IN FIRST PLACE, DONALD'S IN SECOND, WITH GOOFY AND EL HORACE TYING FOR LAST!

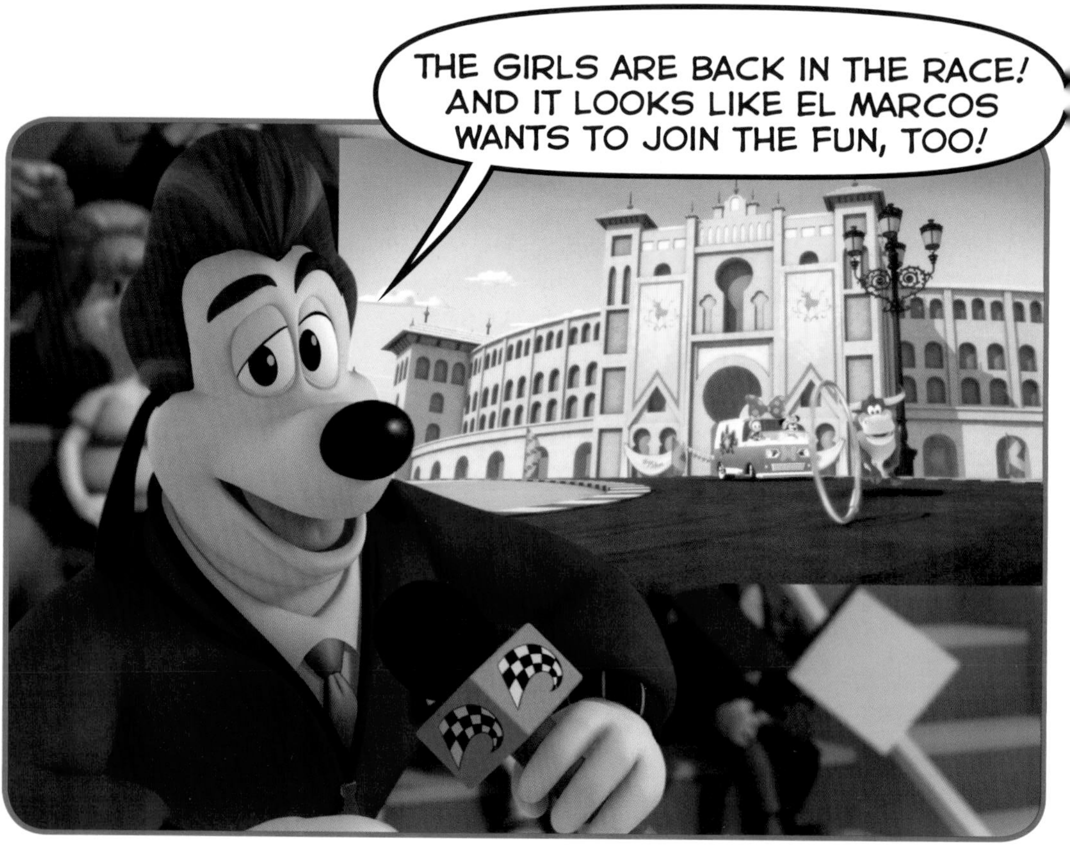
THE GIRLS ARE BACK IN THE RACE! AND IT LOOKS LIKE EL MARCOS WANTS TO JOIN THE FUN, TOO!

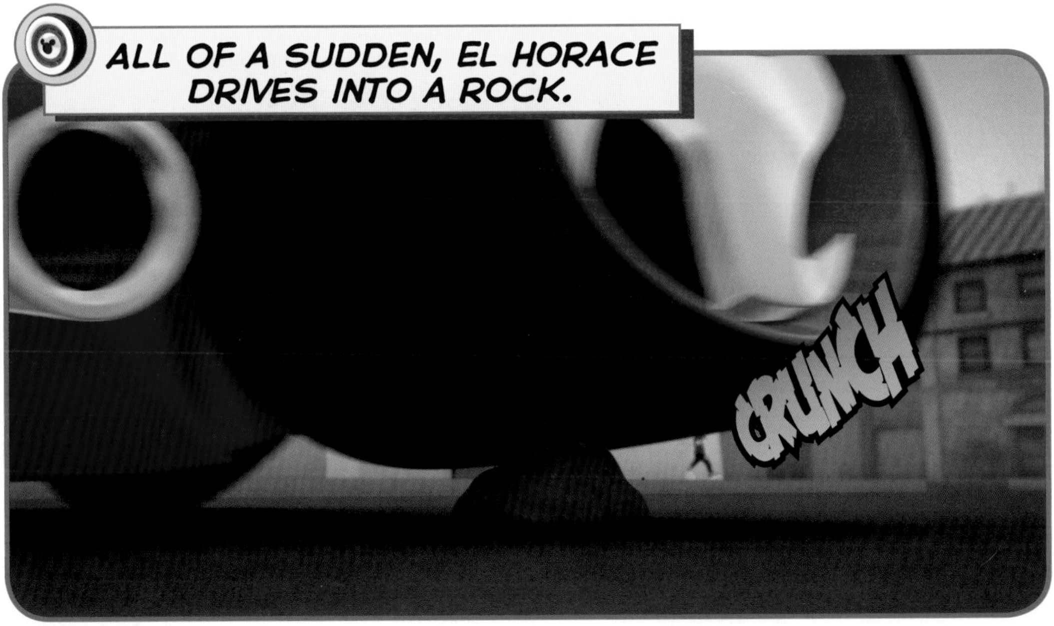
ALL OF A SUDDEN, EL HORACE DRIVES INTO A ROCK.
CRUNCH

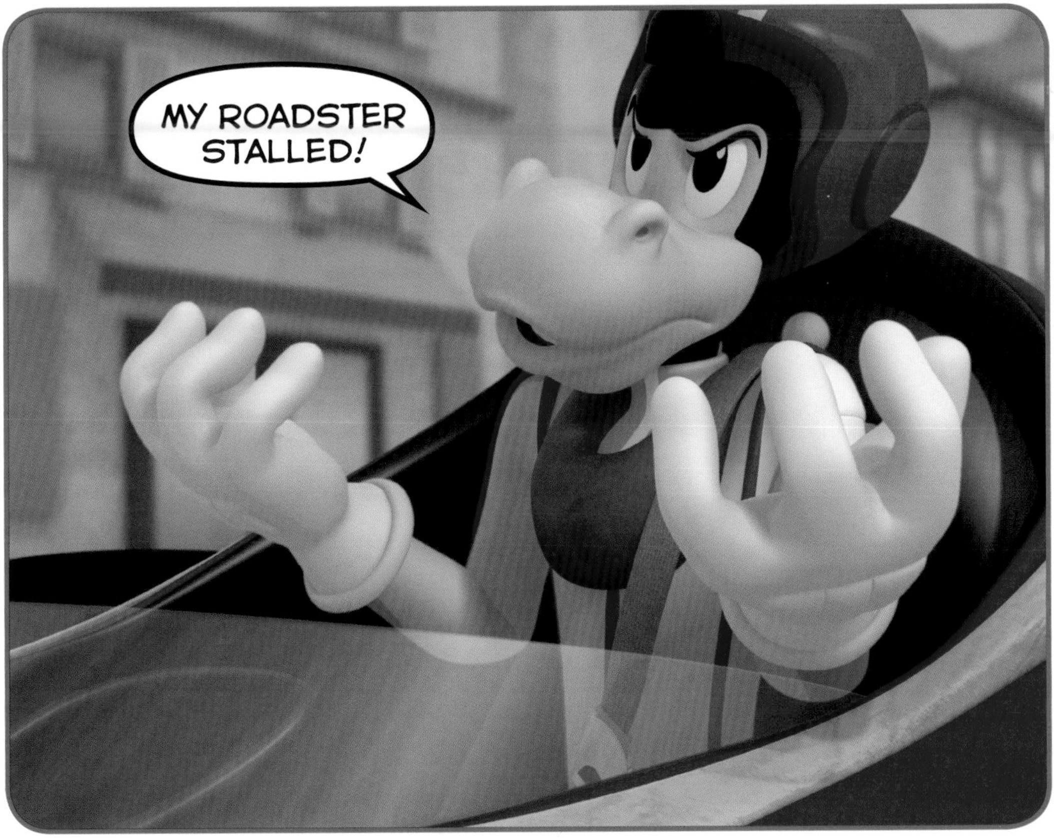
MY ROADSTER STALLED!

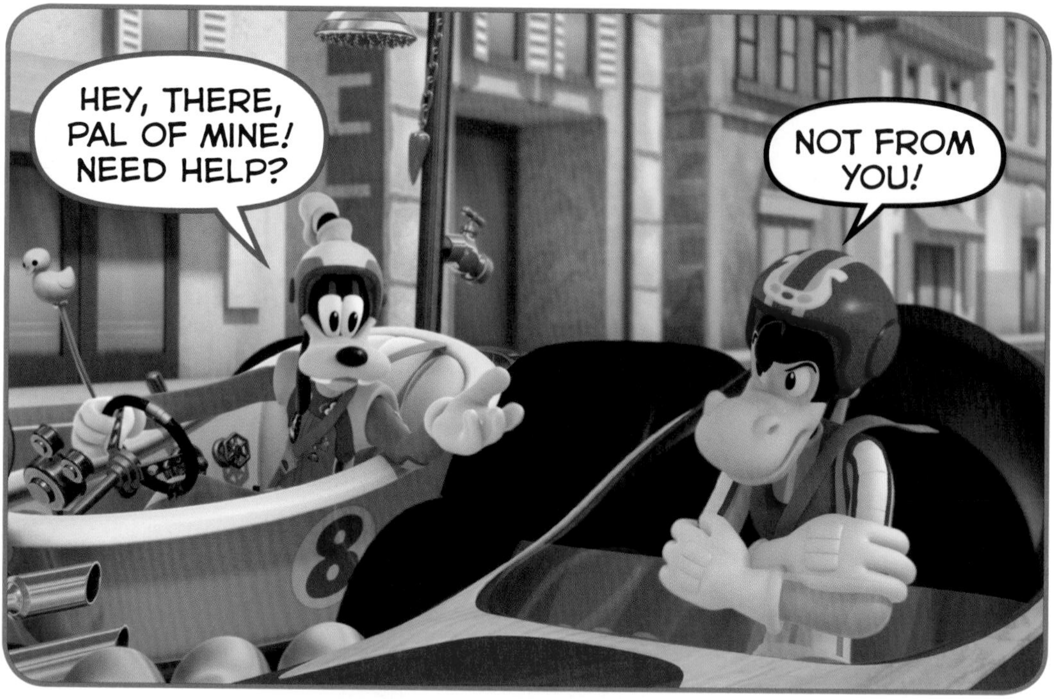
HEY, THERE, PAL OF MINE! NEED HELP?
NOT FROM YOU!

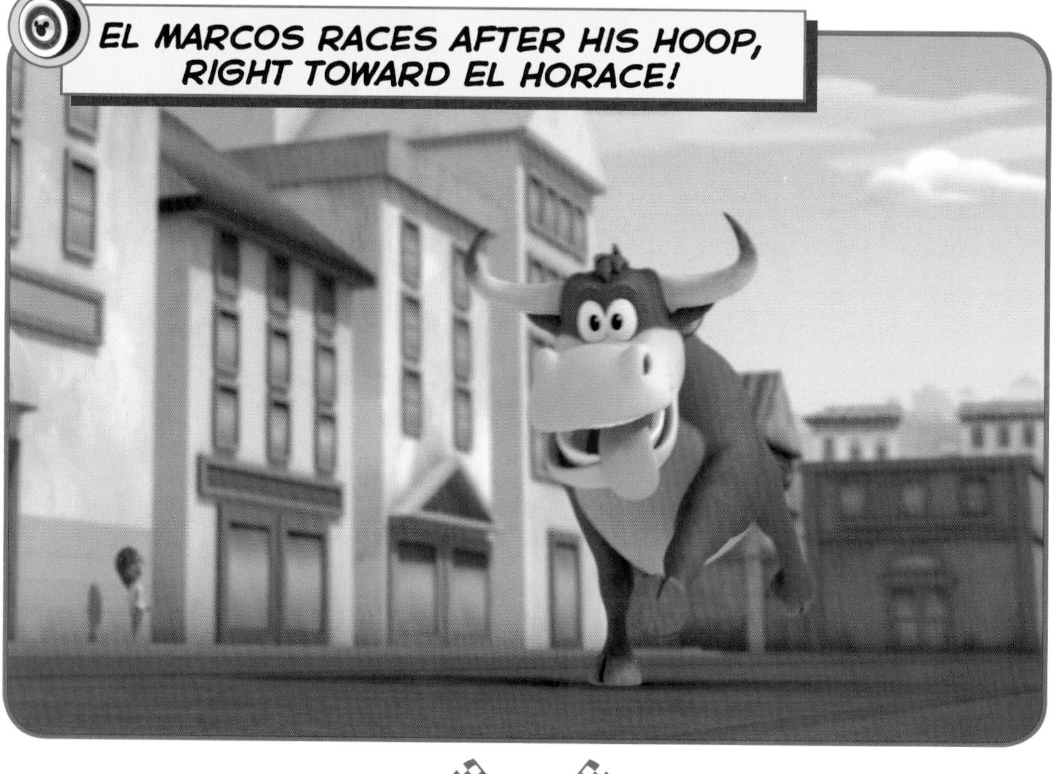
EL MARCOS RACES AFTER HIS HOOP, RIGHT TOWARD EL HORACE!

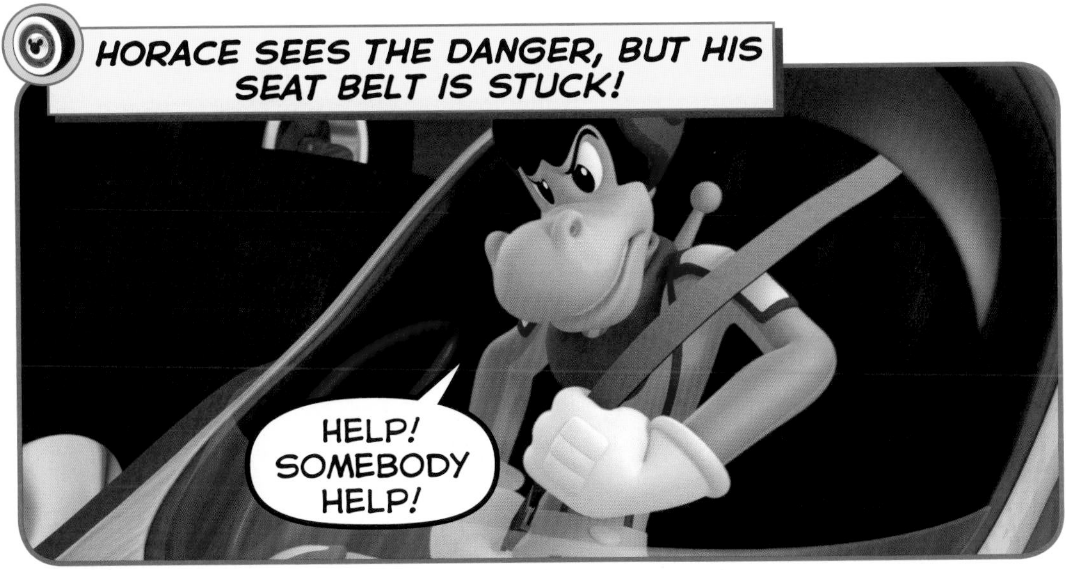
HORACE SEES THE DANGER, BUT HIS SEAT BELT IS STUCK!
HELP! SOMEBODY HELP!

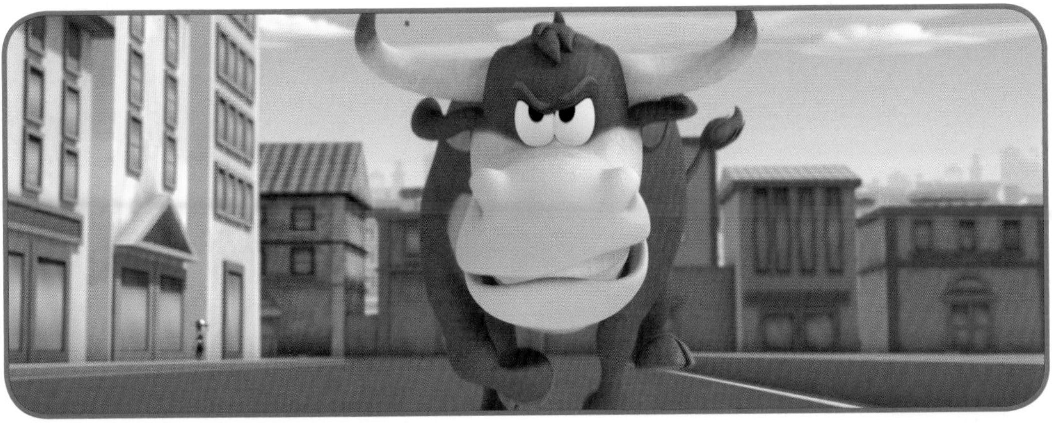

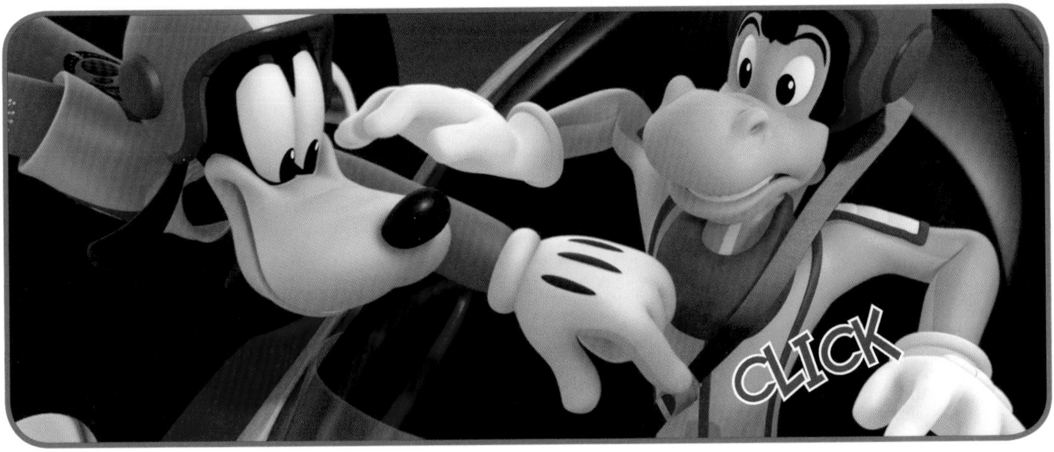
CLICK

GOOFY RESCUES EL HORACE, JUST IN TIME!

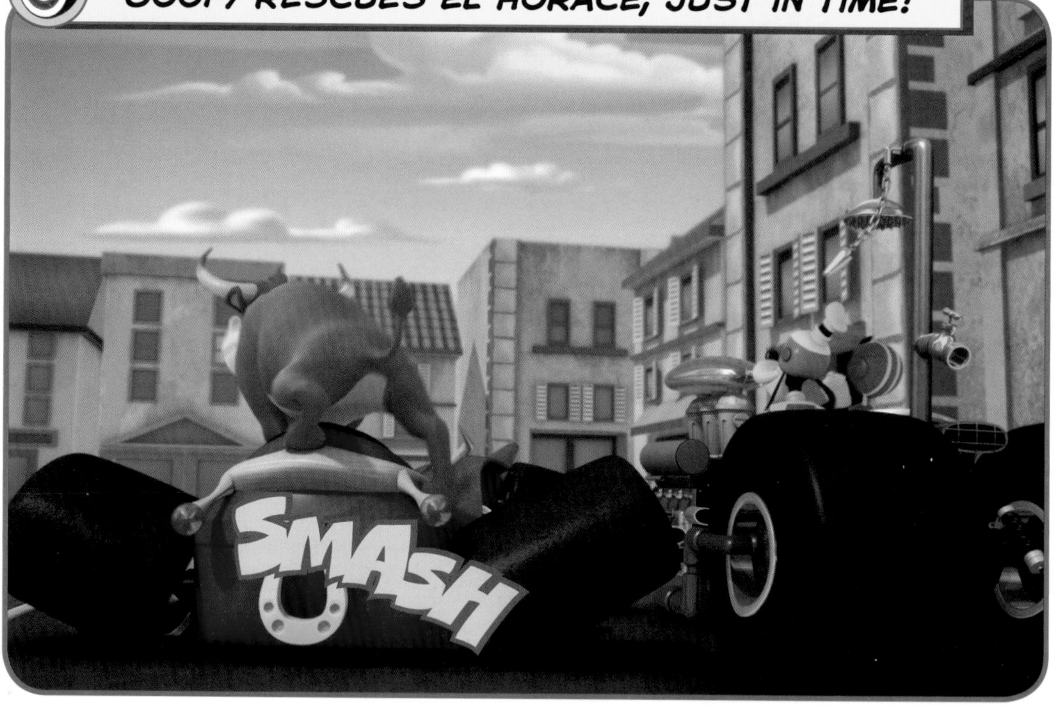
SMASH

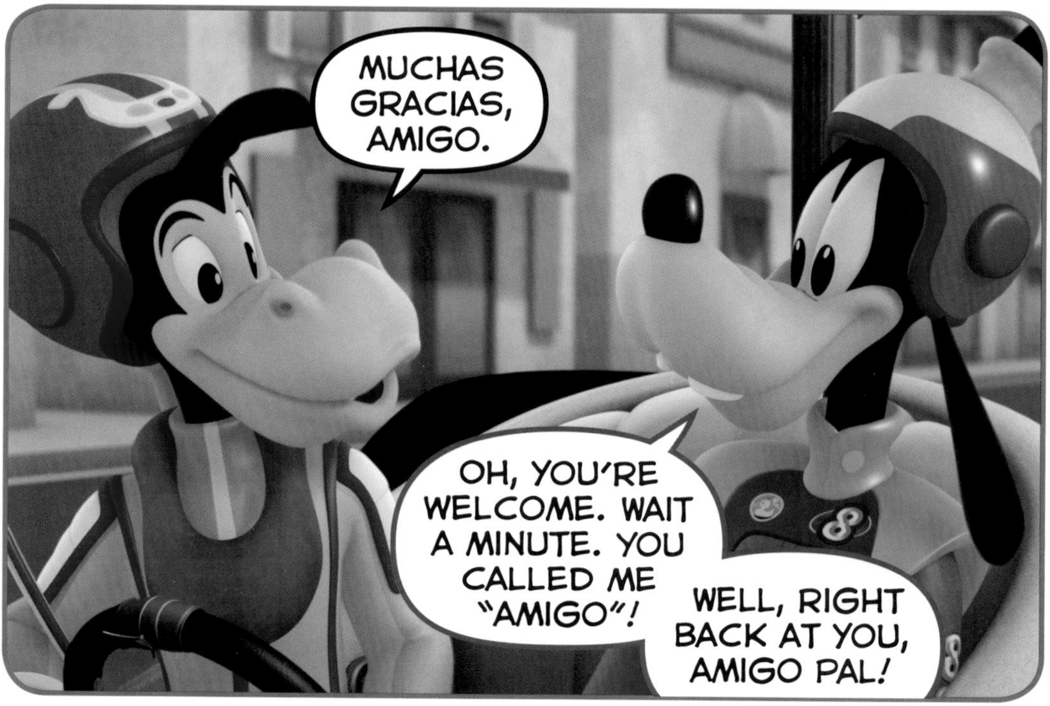
MUCHAS GRACIAS, AMIGO.
OH, YOU'RE WELCOME. WAIT A MINUTE. YOU CALLED ME "AMIGO"!
WELL, RIGHT BACK AT YOU, AMIGO PAL!

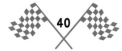

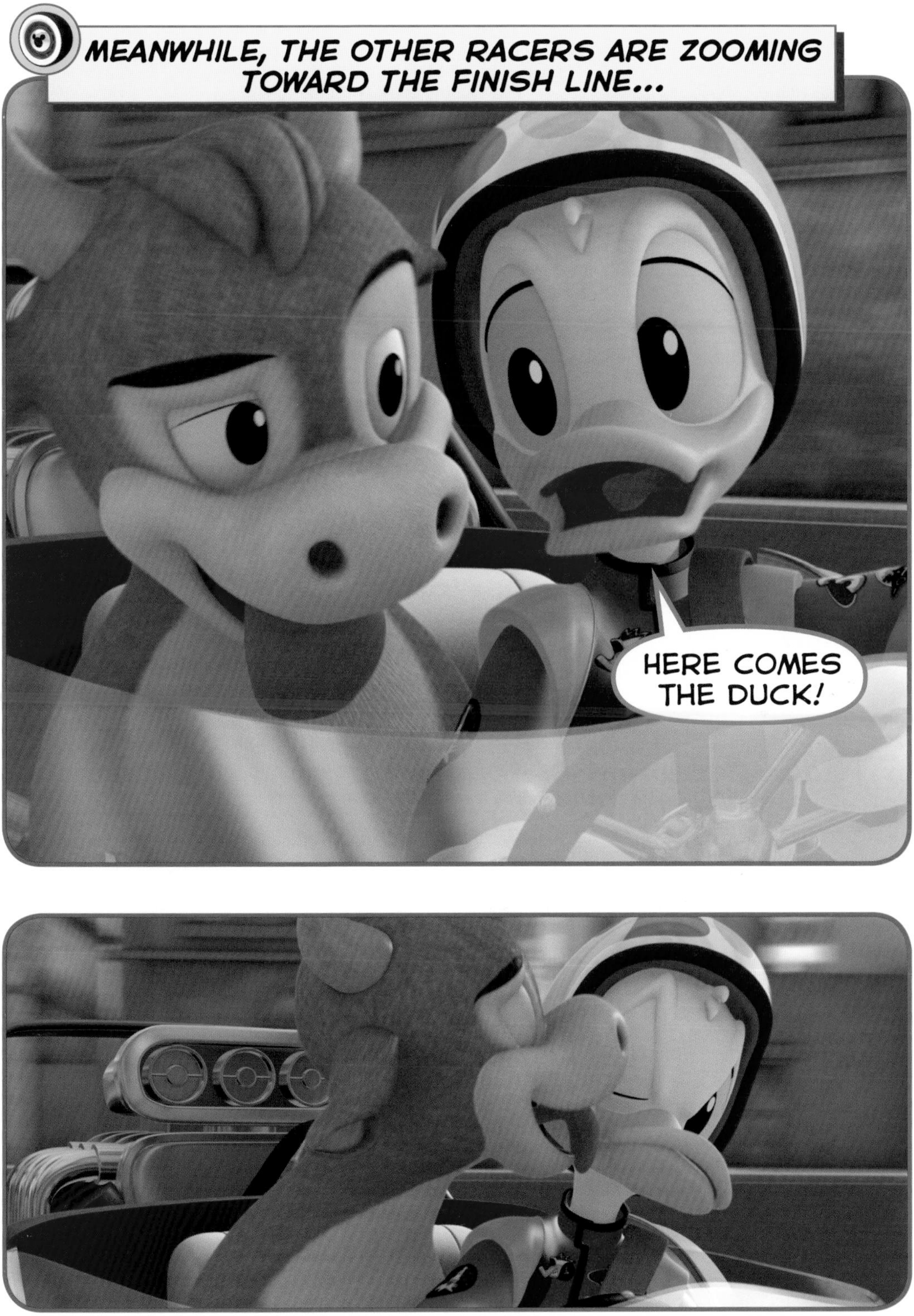
MEANWHILE, THE OTHER RACERS ARE ZOOMING TOWARD THE FINISH LINE...
HERE COMES THE DUCK!

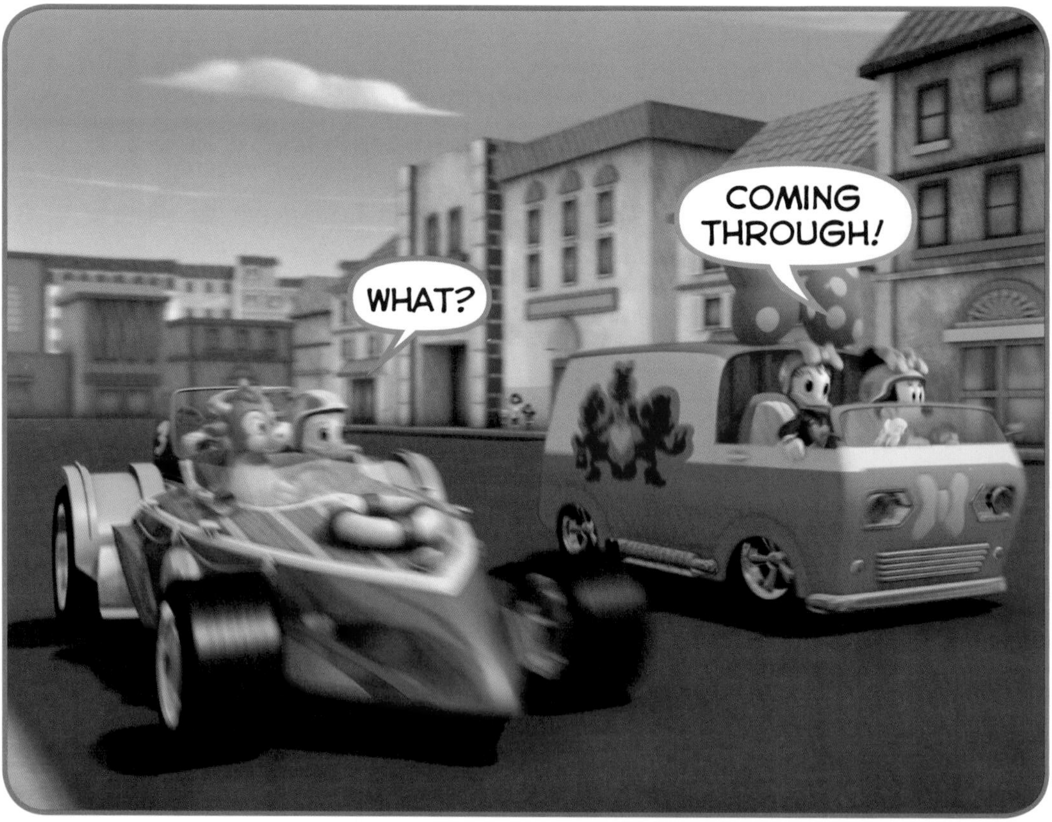
WHAT?
COMING THROUGH!

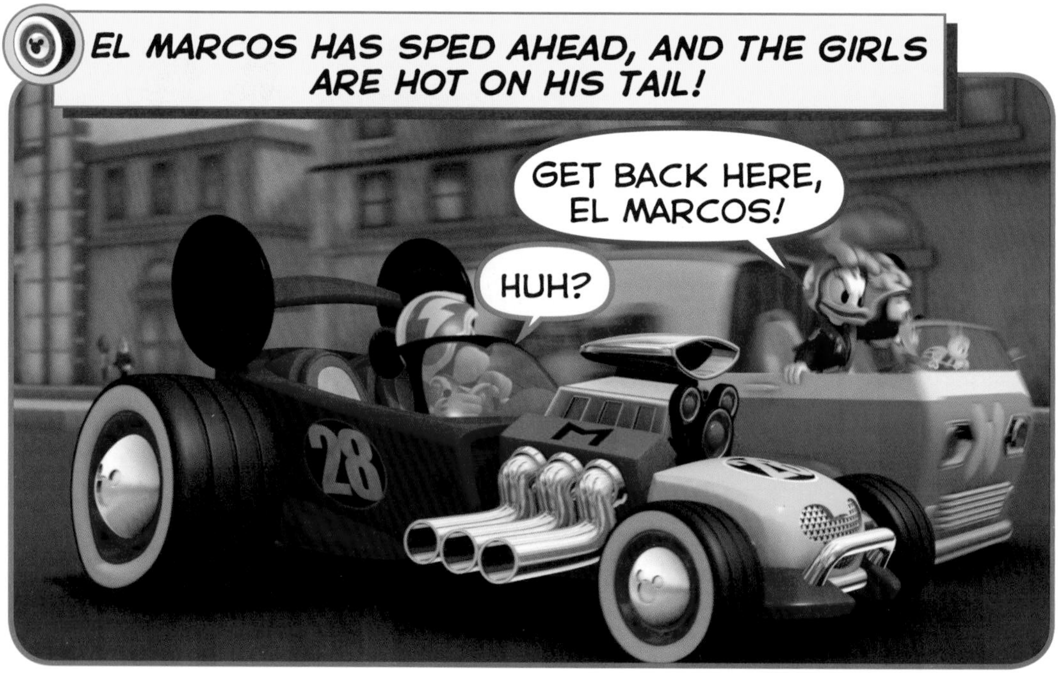
EL MARCOS HAS SPED AHEAD, AND THE GIRLS ARE HOT ON HIS TAIL!
GET BACK HERE, EL MARCOS!
HUH?

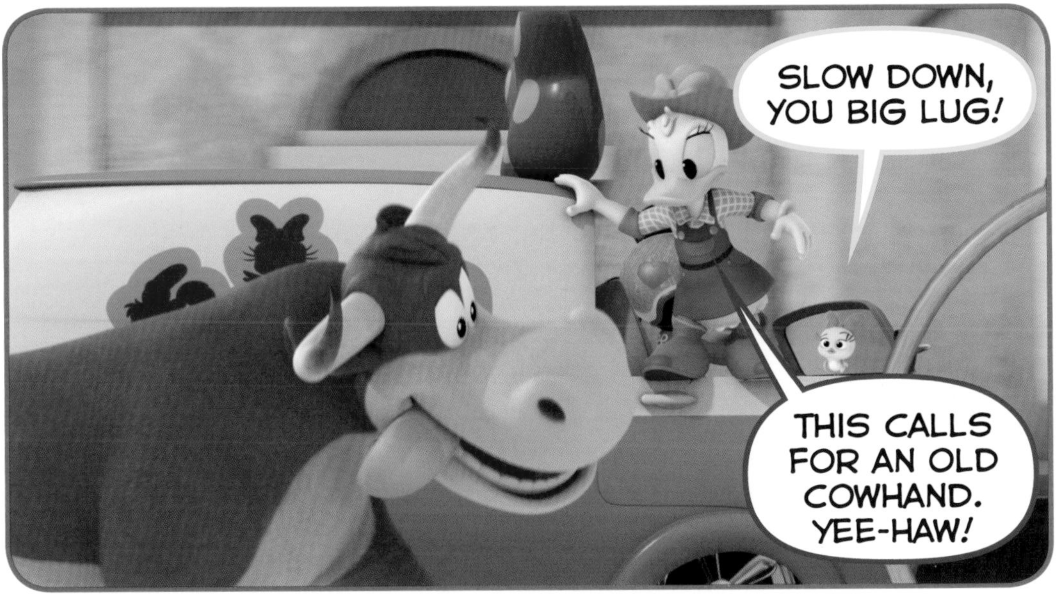
SLOW DOWN, YOU BIG LUG!
THIS CALLS FOR AN OLD COWHAND. YEE-HAW!

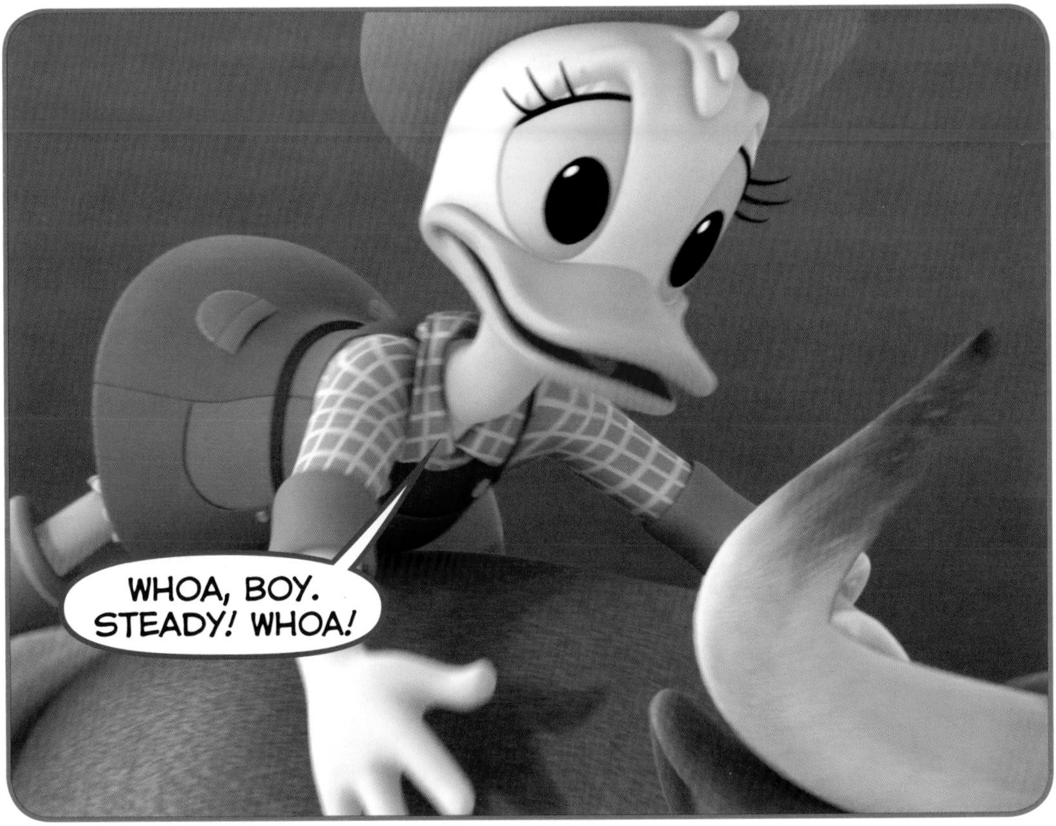
WHOA, BOY. STEADY! WHOA!

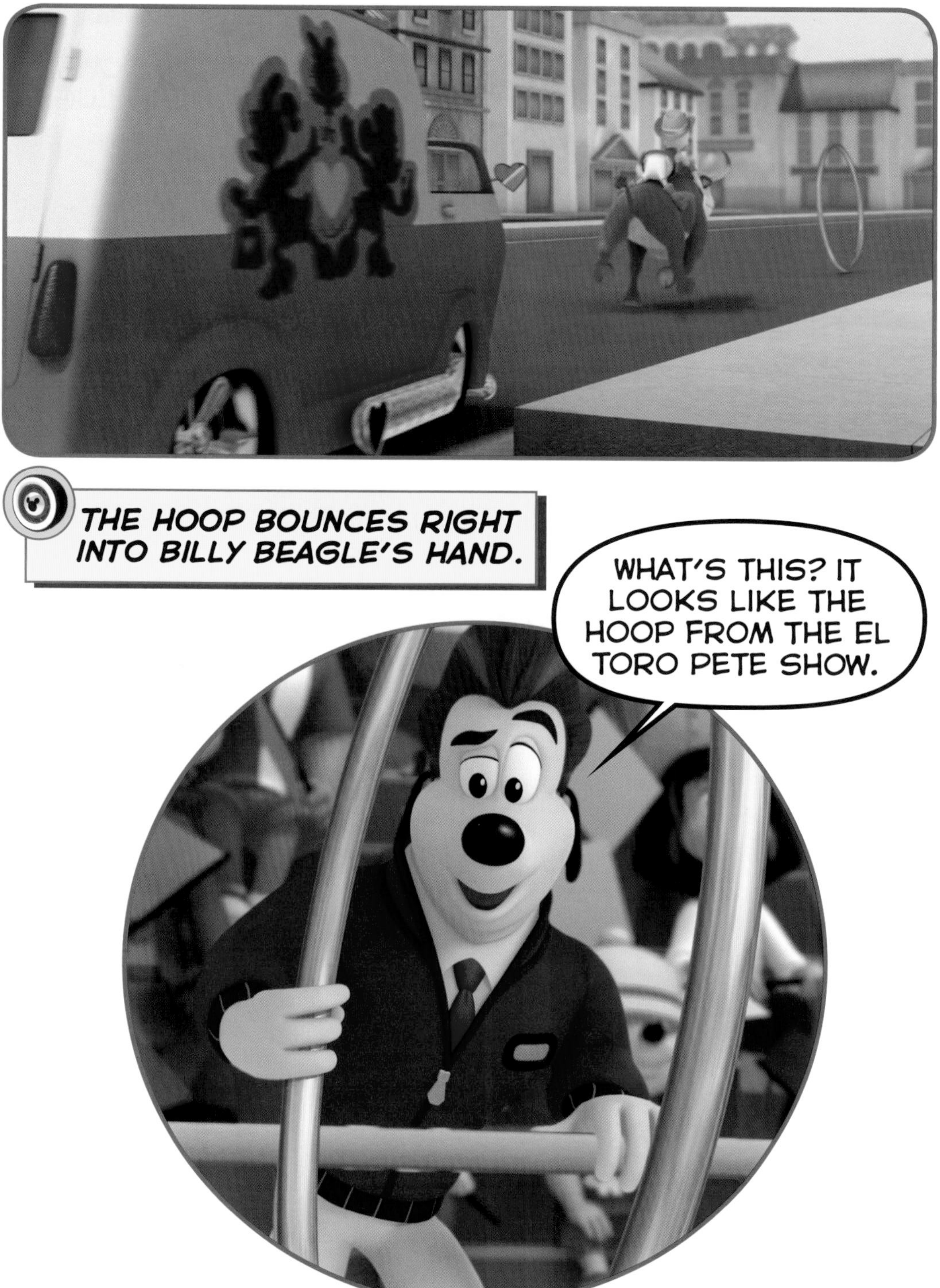
THE HOOP BOUNCES RIGHT INTO BILLY BEAGLE'S HAND.
WHAT'S THIS? IT LOOKS LIKE THE HOOP FROM THE EL TORO PETE SHOW.

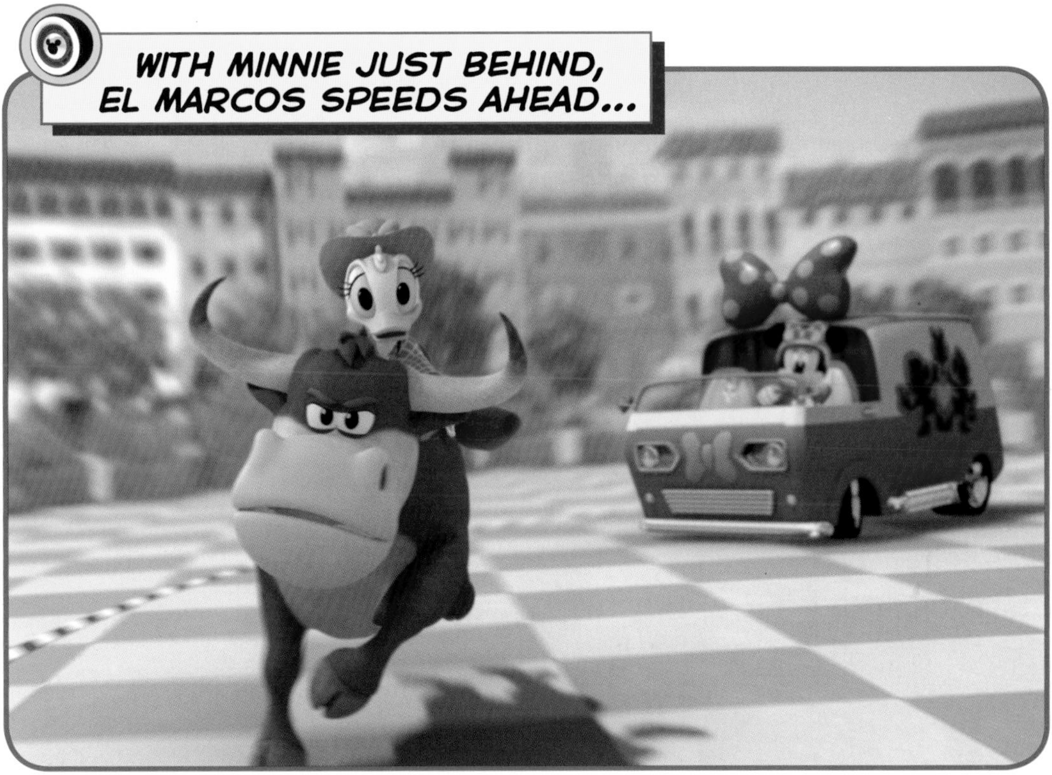
WITH MINNIE JUST BEHIND, EL MARCOS SPEEDS AHEAD...

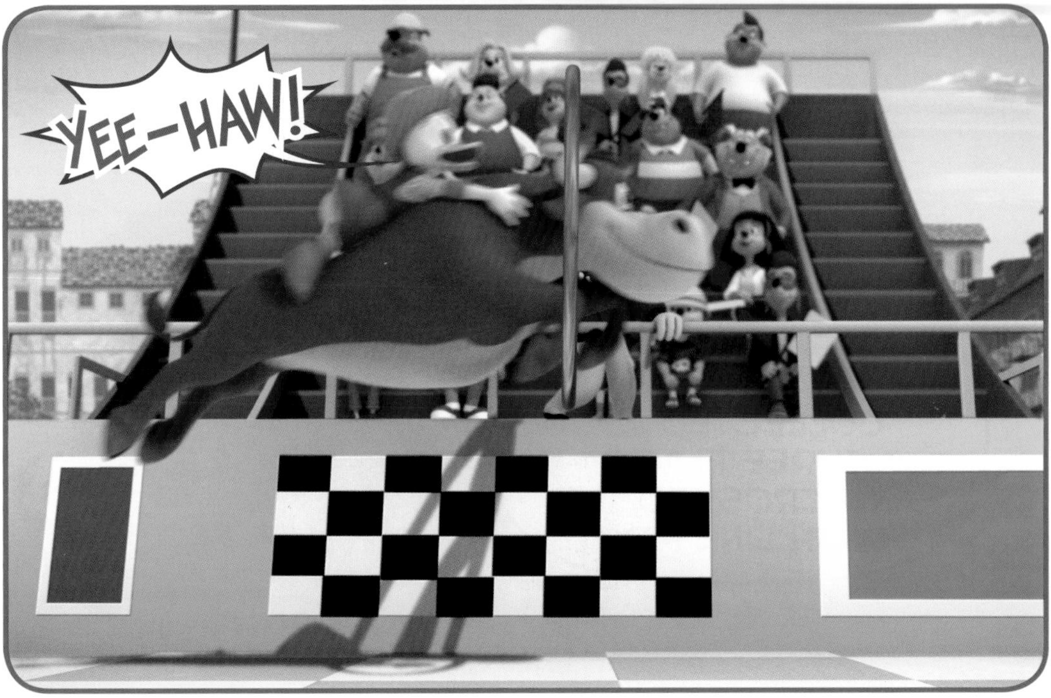
YEE-HAW!

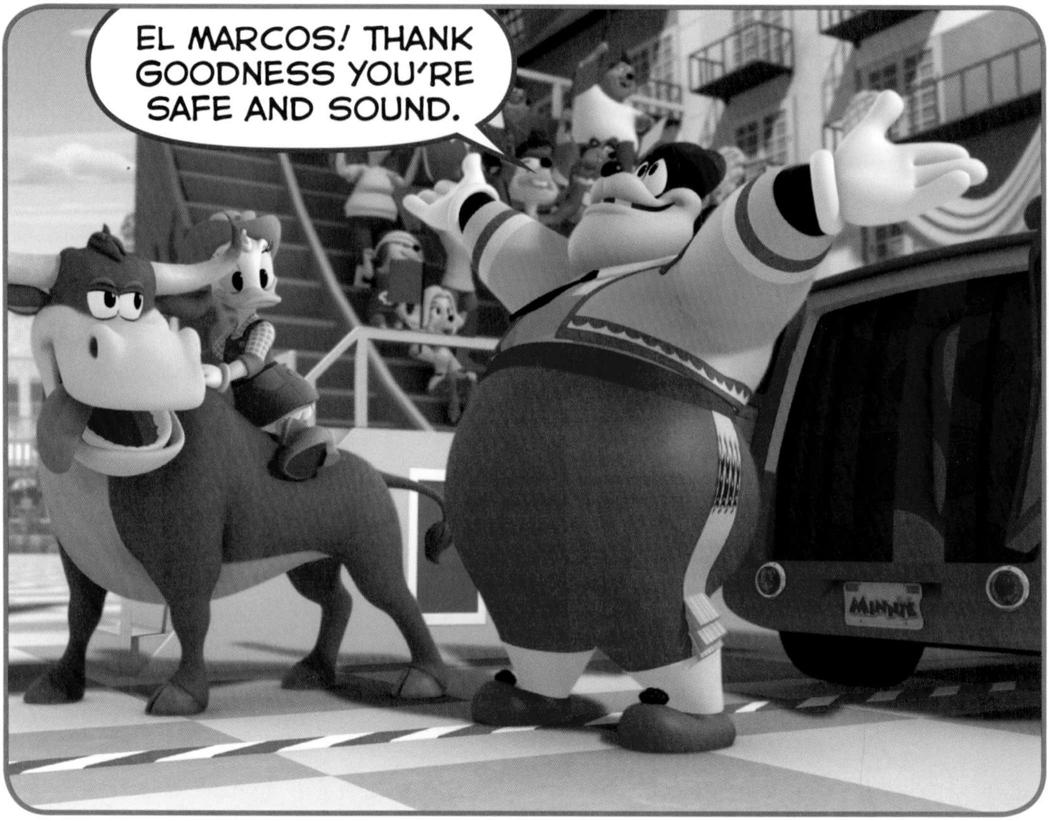
EL MARCOS! THANK GOODNESS YOU'RE SAFE AND SOUND.
MINNIE

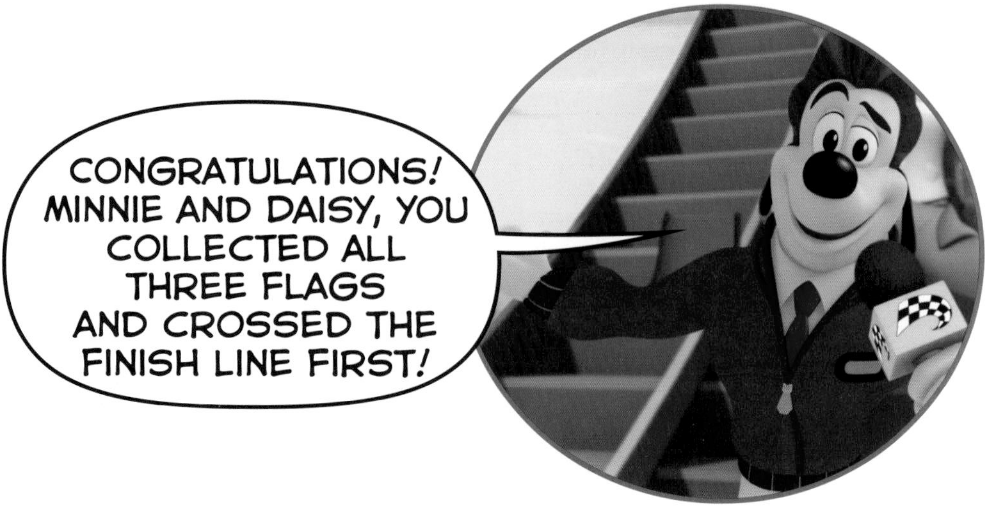
CONGRATULATIONS! MINNIE AND DAISY, YOU COLLECTED ALL THREE FLAGS AND CROSSED THE FINISH LINE FIRST!

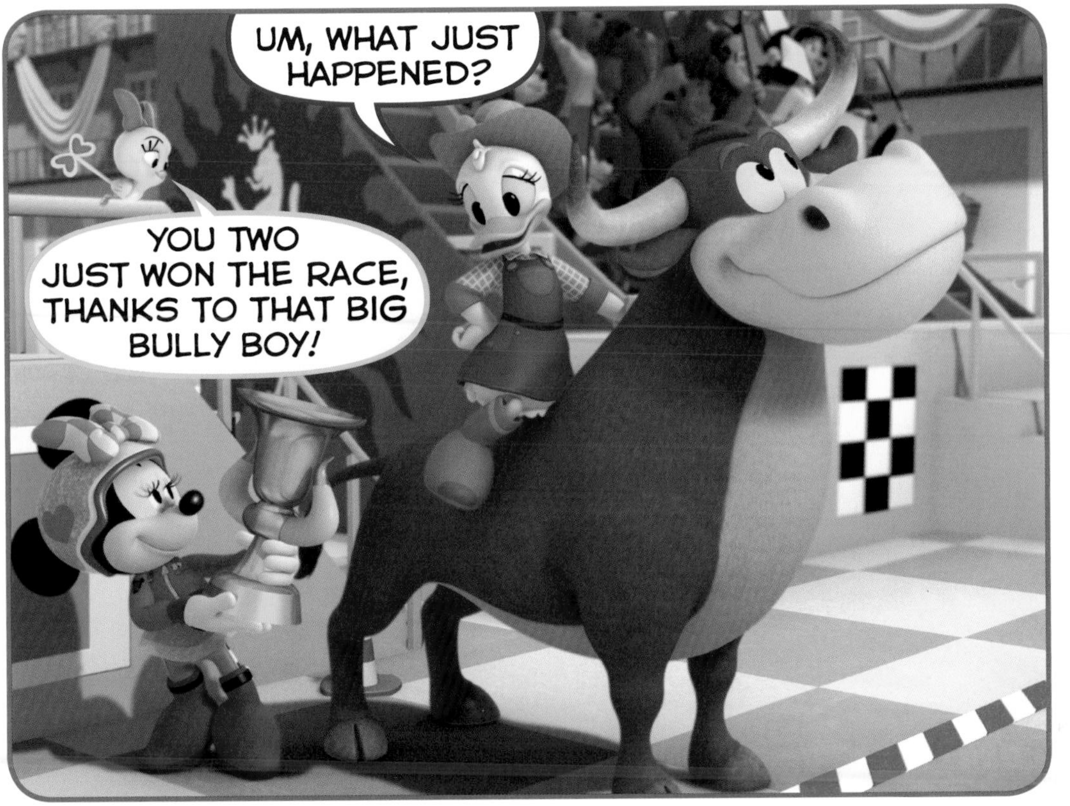
UM, WHAT JUST HAPPENED?
YOU TWO JUST WON THE RACE, THANKS TO THAT BIG BULLY BOY!

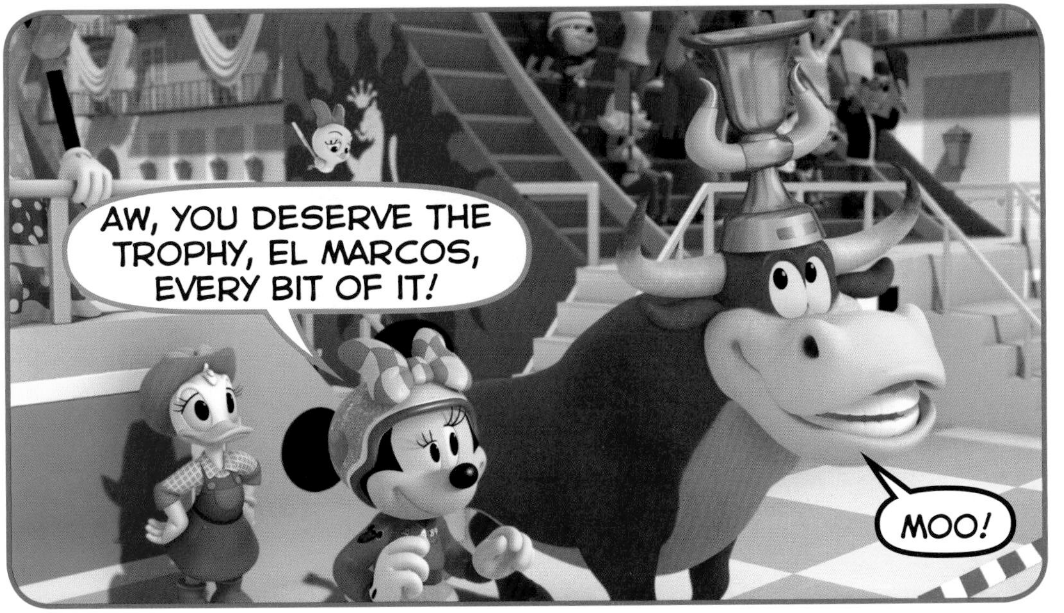
AW, YOU DESERVE THE TROPHY, EL MARCOS, EVERY BIT OF IT!
MOO!

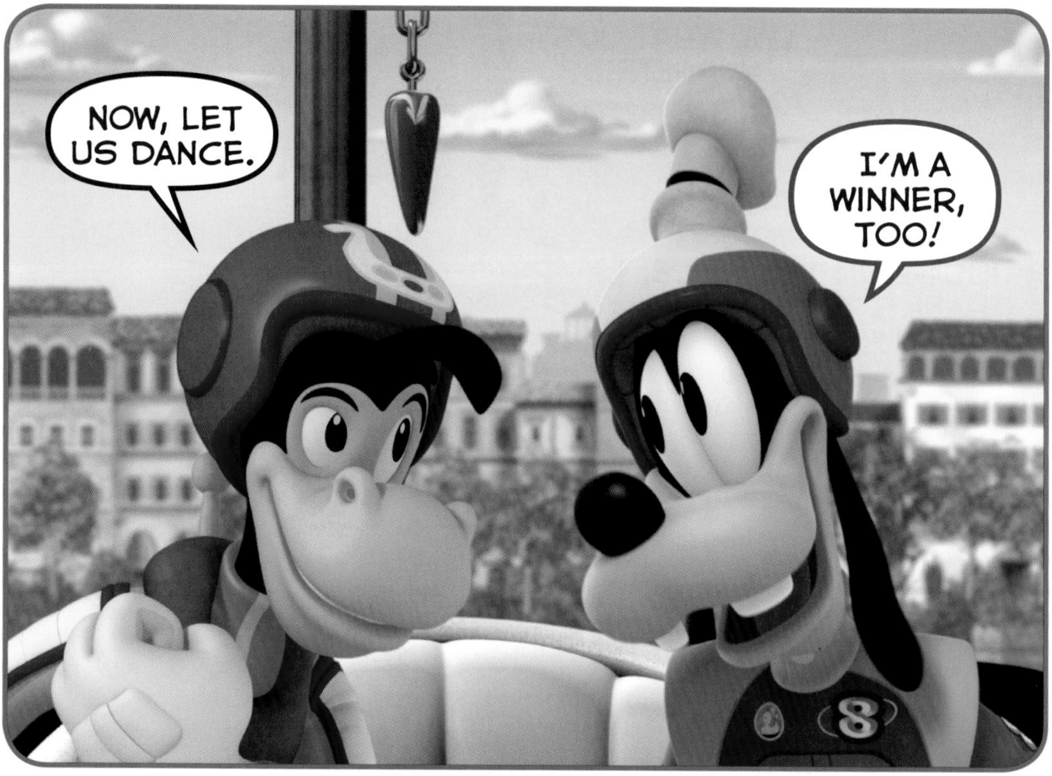
NOW, LET US DANCE.
I'M A WINNER, TOO!

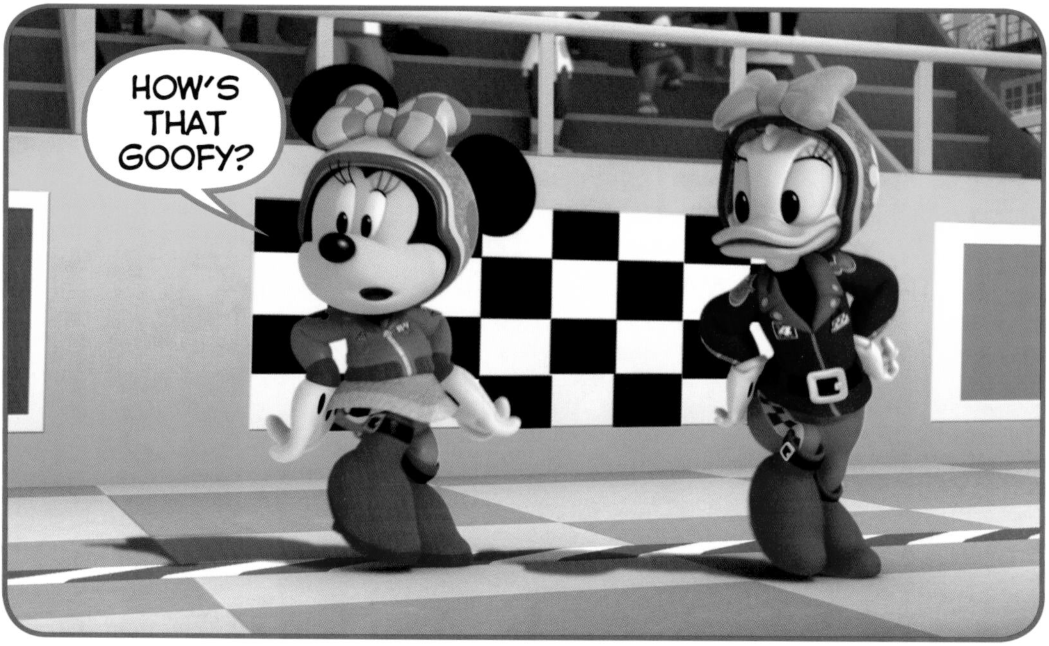
HOW'S THAT GOOFY?

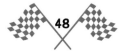

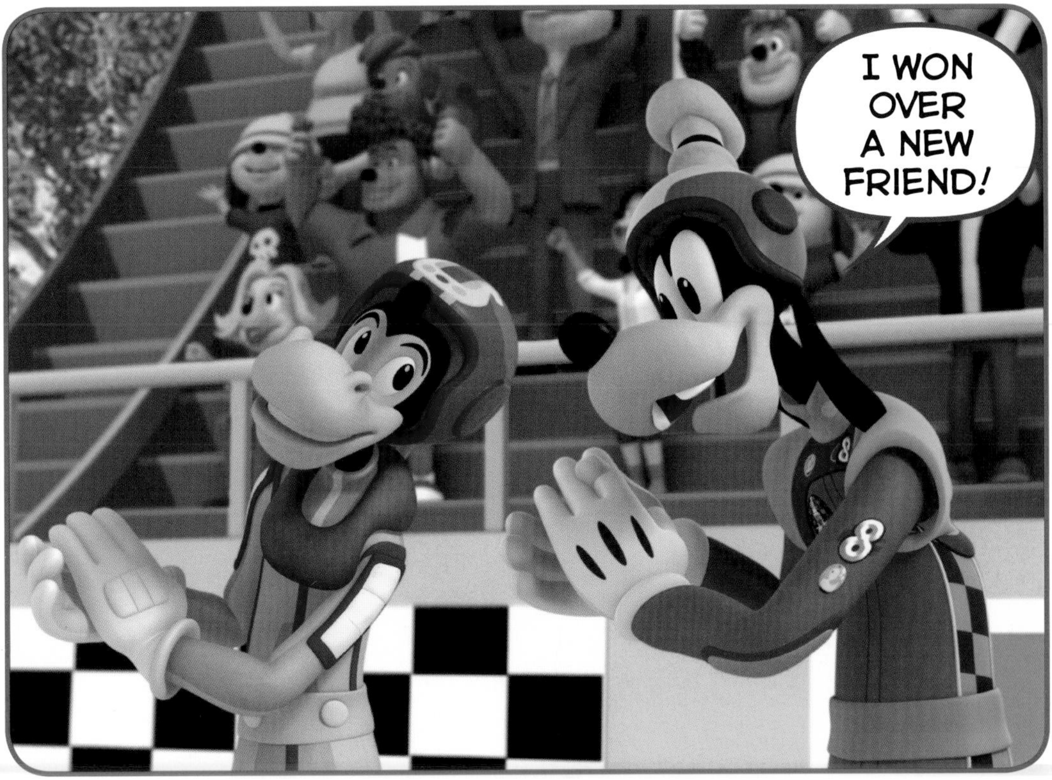
I WON OVER A NEW FRIEND!

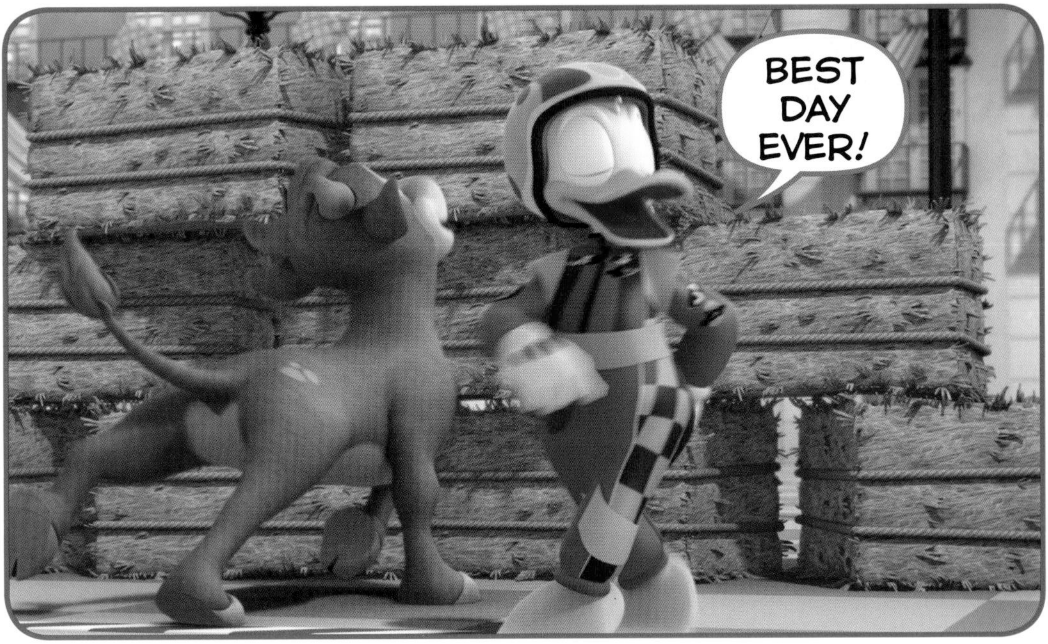
BEST DAY EVER!

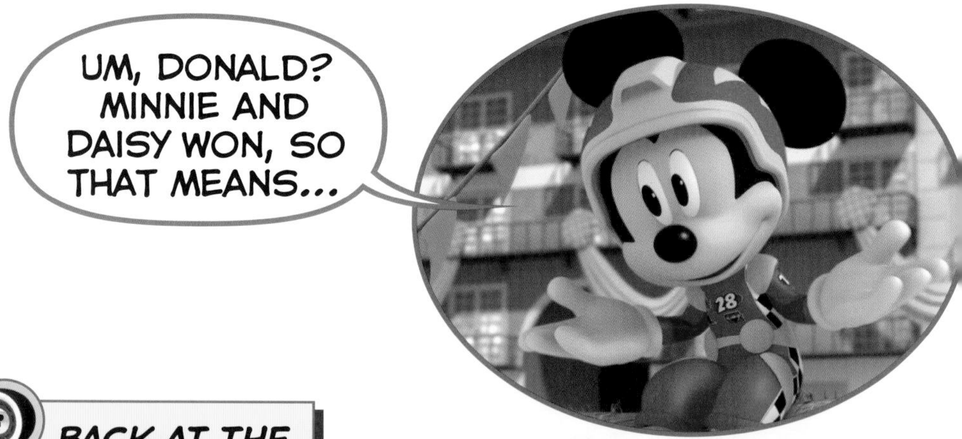
UM, DONALD? MINNIE AND DAISY WON, SO THAT MEANS...

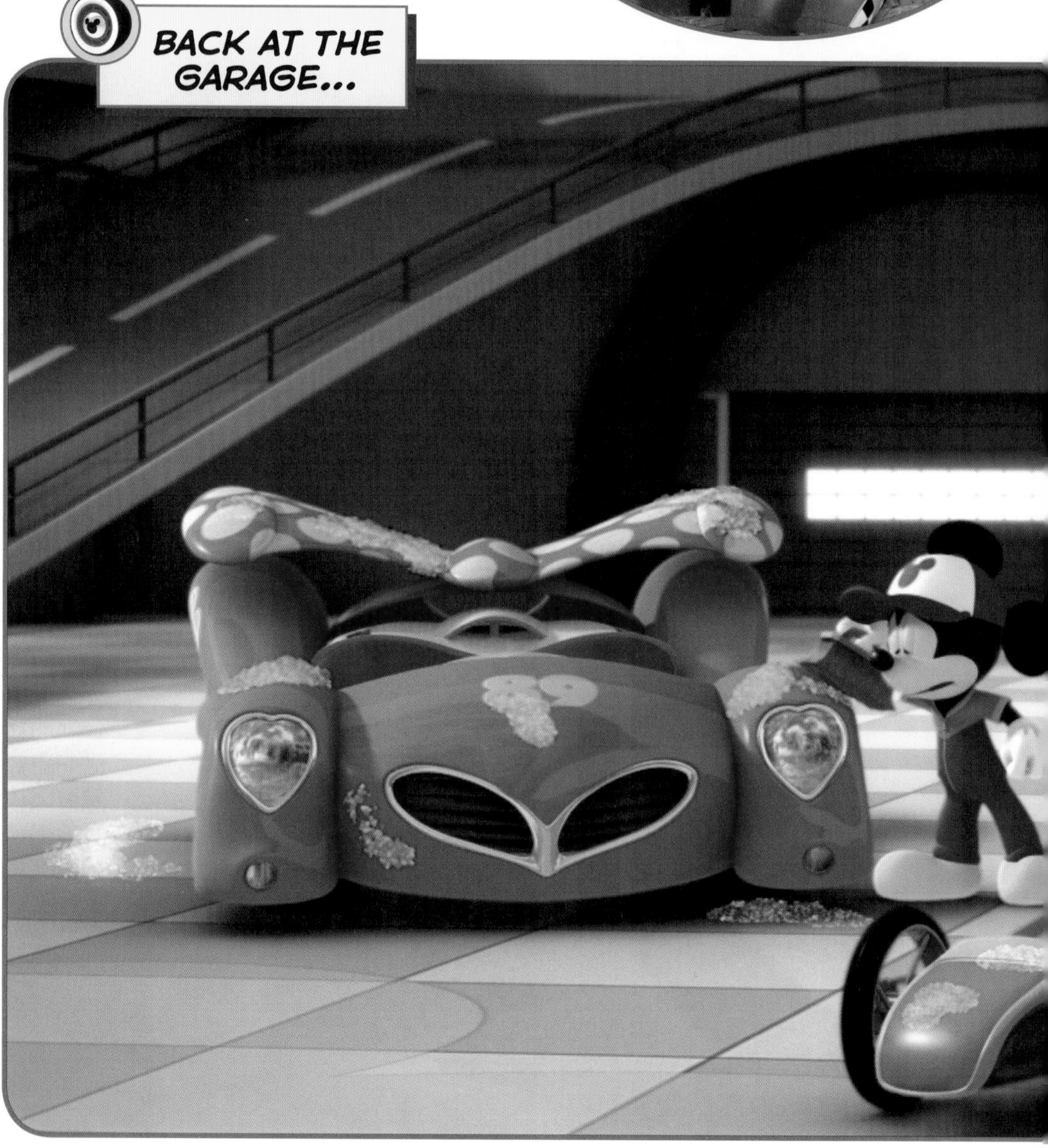
BACK AT THE GARAGE...

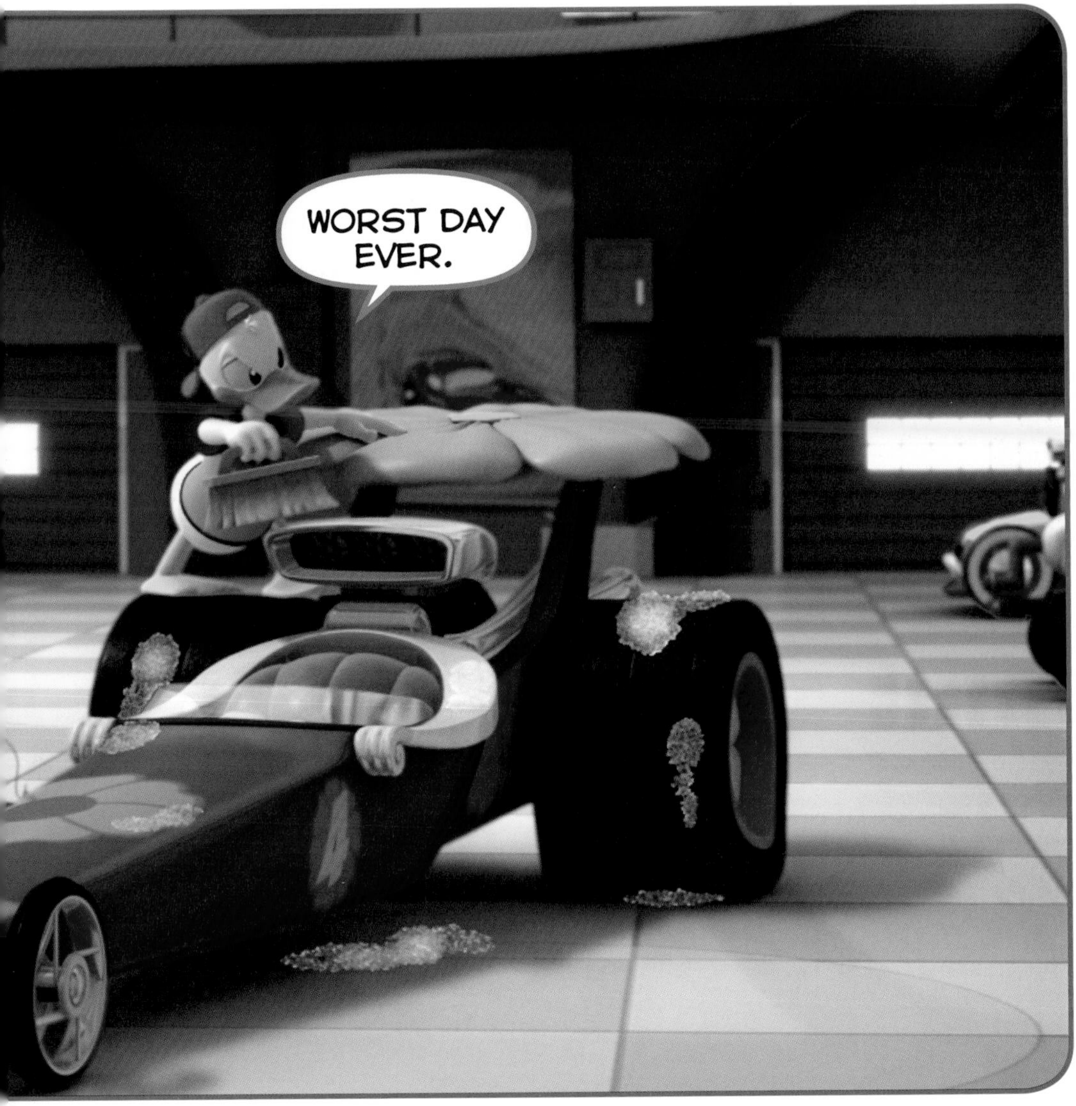
WORST DAY EVER.

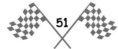

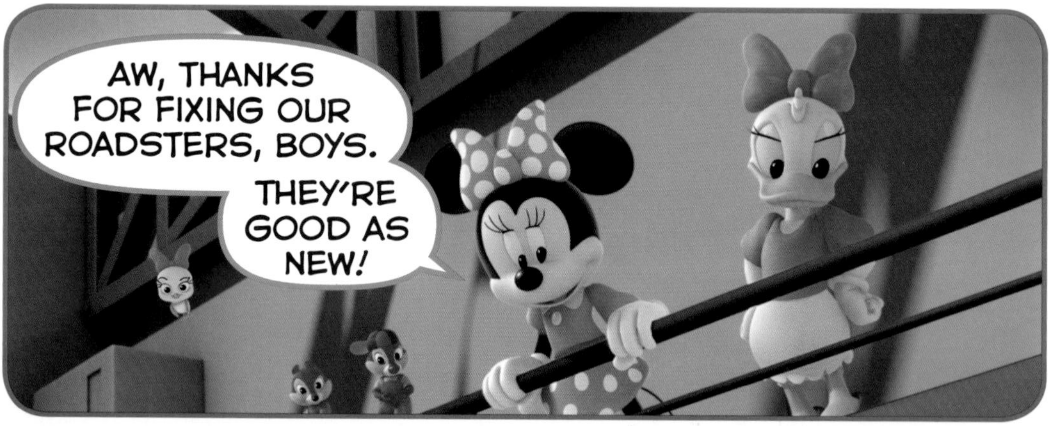
AW, THANKS FOR FIXING OUR ROADSTERS, BOYS.
THEY'RE GOOD AS NEW!

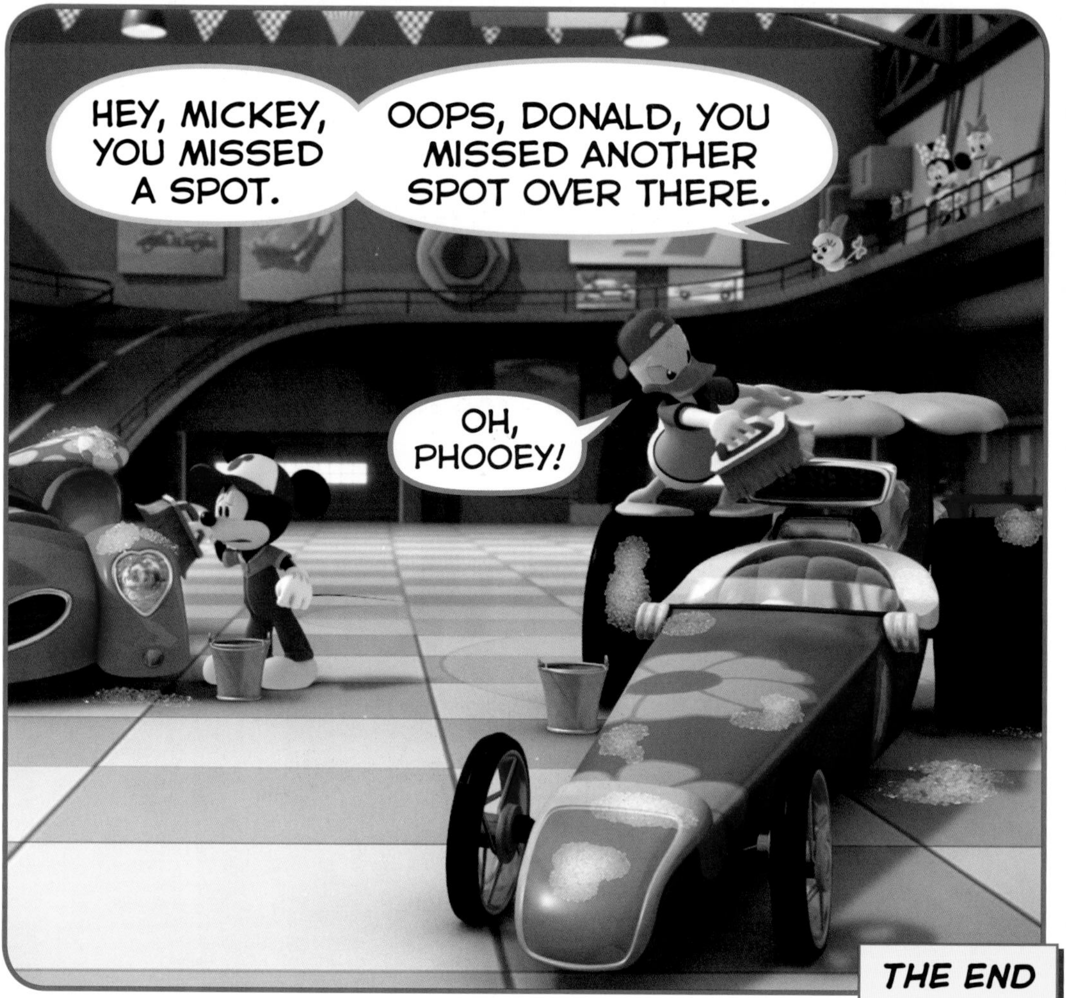
HEY, MICKEY, YOU MISSED A SPOT.
OOPS, DONALD, YOU MISSED ANOTHER SPOT OVER THERE.
OH, PHOOEY!
THE END

Running of the Roadsters

Directed by
Phil Weinstein

Executive Producer
Rob LaDuca

Coexecutive Producer and Supervising Story Editor
Mark Seidenberg

Written by
Mark Drop

Storyboard by
Tom Morgan

DISNEY Junior

ALSO FROM JOE BOOKS

DISNEY

DOC McStuffins

TOY HOSPITAL

Lambie and the McStuffins Babies
CINESTORY COMIC

DISNEY

Vampirina

The Sleepover
CINESTORY COMIC